The Forest and the Trees

A Medical Novel

Benjamin W. Strong, MD

PublishAmerica
Baltimore

First printing

The characters in this novel are fictional and any resemblance to real persons living or dead is purely coincidental. The medical procedures, complications, and disease entities portrayed herein are all accurately accounted and described. Much condensation and simplification was required for readability, however, and this work in no way constitutes an appropriate medical reference.

ISBN: 1-4137-0979-6
PUBLISHED BY
PUBLISHAMERICA, LLLP.
www.publishamerica.com
Baltimore

Printed in the United States of America

Dedication

To my wife, Christina, who made this book possible (and not to my parents, who have supported me in everything but this).

The Forest and the Trees
A Medical Novel

It was the big day. Midlin stretched out his hand to press '2' and the crisp crease of his new white coat caught his eye; he breathed deeply the scent of new, newly shampooed carpet as the elevator door slid shut with a hermetic hiss. His spirits and the elevator rose as he reveled in his new surroundings, and his mind ranged briefly over the not-so-brief ordeal he had endured to get here. There had been years of tag-team lecturing that had left his head whirling with formulas, charts, and graphs and his other end aching from prolonged hours of sitting. There had been sensitivity sessions, liability sessions, and sessions on interviewing the homosexual, the drug user, the wife beater and the firestarter. He had climbed mountains of paperwork, crossed valleys of insecurity and forded rivers of urine and blood. Despite the outdoor buffet, yesterday's orientation had been no picnic with its onslaught of protocol, policy, and precautions. But at last here he was in a veritable health palace, he thought: smart, sensitive, and initiated.

The loudspeaker intruded rudely on his dreamy thoughts, much like his mother's shrill voice on schooldays and with the same ultimate effect on his mood. The timing of the thing was surreal and tragic, like Romeo's dying as Juliet awakens. A chime sounded softly as the elevator doors opened and gave Midlin his first glimpse of the emergency room even as the overhead speaker announced his very first cardiopulmonary arrest in that same location. Looking across the hall to the intake bays, he saw a gurney bearing a bluish-gray, androgynous blob wheel to a stop and then immediately disappear from view as a horde of technicians, nurses, patient aids, and paramedics surrounded the beleaguered figure. Midlin's earlier assessment of himself was shaken severely as he realized that he was in fact only sensitive enough to see that he was neither smart nor initiated. A jumbled list of facts ran through his head, an unbidden and unconscious grasping for familiarity. Midlin felt terror grip his heart as he realized that although able to list the sting of the Trinidade scorpion as a cause of pancreatitis, the Reduvid bug as the vector for Chaga's disease, and the amoeba Nigleria as the culprit causing meningitis in cliff divers he didn't know a single fact of use to anyone in this situation. The one thing he was sure of was that he had no idea how to proceed. Without further thought on the matter (except a brief reminiscence on the spread of sleeping sickness by the tse-tse fly), Midlin slipped past the open door to the bay and into an adjacent stairwell, assuring he would be the last to arrive at the first arrest of the year. He felt the floor vibrate as the approaching code team threw shadows on the opposite wall, and the door closed behind him just in time to prevent anyone from detecting his flight.

It took a long minute for them to pass, a minute that stretched on and on for Midlin as he grew more embarrassed by his behavior with every second that passed. As the last white coat and stethoscope flapped and swung by he was sufficiently shamed to follow immediately, and in his now-dejected state of mind he opened the door and entered the hallway with his gaze fixed firmly on the floor. It was because of this that he bounced off the rotund straggler and his first sight of her was from below. She was huffing and puffing as though about to make a go at a brick house but she was still able to gasp out a reprimand.

"Come on, come on. You have to run to these. And watch where you're going."

Midlin found himself hoisted onto his feet and propelled through the ER door and his newly acquired shame was replaced with a now-familiar feeling of ineptitude. There was a brief moment when he felt panic rising in his throat when he thought that not enough time had elapsed for events to run their course and for his inadequate attentions to become unnecessary. There still seemed to be no order in the room and it was now so full of people and bustle that Midlin's relative immobility was all the more conspicuous. He cast a glance at the unfortunate bruise-colored patient hoping to see the telltale Winterbottom's sign of sleeping sickness and when there was none to be seen he sadly realized his diagnostic offerings were at an end. There was no information to be gleaned whatsoever from that lifeless lump of flesh, who to Midlin looked no less dead than Julius Caeser. Before his inability could cause the embarrassing scene he had initially envisioned and hoped to avoid, however, his fat benefactor shoved past him and Midlin was relieved to see that with her present no one would look to him for direction.

"Give me two large-bore peripherals, labs, ABG, O2, EKG, suction, intubation tray with a 7.0 tube, and a central line kit."

Her words paralyzed every last person in the room and Midlin saw pensive expressions all around as people considered whether or not their current activities were on the fat woman's list. Chaos gradually returned, however, and people resumed opening sterile containers, sticking needles in the lifeless limbs on the table, and pounding on the patient's equally lifeless chest. The fat woman, clearly satisfied that this pause had represented an organizational interlude of unparalleled efficacy, now strode to the head of the bed and displaced a number of residents already gathered there. An impending intubation drew residents like pigeons to seed, but the fat woman scattered them like a mischievous boy in the park.

"It's got to be the first shot this time, folks. Sorry." Saying this she lifted the 7.0 from the tray and the disgruntled crowd murmured and made way.

"Give me an oral airway. Ambu bag with 100%. Good. Now 20 of etomidate, 10 of vecuronium, and have the ventilator ready."

Midlin watched as an oral airway, a laryngoscope and then a tube were inserted into the patient's windpipe with crisp, military efficiency. He marveled at the fat woman's calm and detached demeanor during the whole procedure, but this only lasted until he had pushed his way to the head of the bed next to a sweating, chest-compressing paramedic on his right and a brownnosing medical student on the left (positioned near the head so as to immediately execute the fat woman's next order). From this new location he was able to better perceive the fat woman's sweating brow and clenched teeth and he was able to better hear her muttering fiercely just under her breath as she worked. Abruptly she relaxed, straightened, and stepped back while withdrawing the stiffening stylet from the endotracheal tube with a flourish. The tube was attached to a waiting ventilator by a number of eager hands, and the bluish chest on the gurney began to rise and fall in a pathetic mimicry of breathing.

At this point Midlin mentally noted that he had as yet performed no useful task, and on the heels of that came the realization that there seemed to be no such task he could perform. There was a flurry of hands and needles over the groins that resembled a miniature Errol Flynn climax, the iodine- and blood-soaked chest was plastered with EKG leads looking like early stars in a Hawaiian sunset, and the limbs were all stretched into impossible positions as personnel probed for venous and arterial offerings. All of it was done faster, more efficiently, and more adeptly than Midlin could have done it and none of it made him feel any less useless. He made a desperate glance to the head of the bed where he saw the obsequious medical student with a nasogastric tube performing the last available simple task. Sighing inwardly he successively yielded space to those better able to contribute until he found himself seated against the wall on a padded stool where a mop-wielding janitor asked him to lift his feet. He consoled himself thinking that at least from this new vantage point he could watch the fat woman run the remainder of the code and better appreciate her marvelous efficiency.

She was incredible. She seemed to Midlin to defy the laws of matter and space, diapedesing in amoeboid fashion amongst the IV poles, wire leads, and tubing that now emanated from the patient while pressing monitor buttons, checking pulses, and auscultating and percussing cavities. She barked orders, adjusted drip rates, administered medications and placed catheters without once taking her eyes from the monitor suspended in the corner. There was no hesitation in her responses to the apparently indecipherable scribble of the EKG, and she recited her resuscitation mantra with a faraway look in her eyes that reflected her total comfort with the situation. At last Midlin felt a general release of tension in the room, and a second later even he knew enough to be relieved when the fat woman announced "Normal sinus rhythm."

Although the shapeless but colorful mass on the table was now sporting a normal sinus rhythm Midlin had seen no actual change in the appearance of the patient since his and Midlin's asynchronous arrivals on the scene. The patient had not spoken or moved, and was far less likely to do so now that he was pharmaceutically paralyzed with a garden hose in his windpipe and tubing tethers on his limbs. The only signs of life Midlin could see were on the monitors, where numerous tracings and beepings demonstrated objectively to the world the success of the fat woman's ministrations. There was a jovial atmosphere in the room and congratulatory gestures and words were seen and heard all around but Midlin shared in none of it. This was partly because he knew no one in the room and partly because he was ashamed of being proven woefully inept on this his first day, but more even than these things Midlin felt isolated by his feeling that what they had done was not so laudable. Looking into the open, glassy eyes of the bluish-gray, unresponsive patient Midlin could simply not picture this man returning the loving gaze of his wife or watching his child graduate and he could not convince himself that this was a man snatched from the jaws of death. Midlin thought he looked more like a piece of meat left on the counter for a week and truly saw no cause for celebration but he attributed his doubts to his own lack of experience and remained silent.

The gurney had been wheeled less than an inch on its journey to the ICU when it was halted by a sharp cry from the fat woman. Clearly Midlin had not been the only one to notice the patient's fixed stare and now he watched as the fat woman bounced across the room while producing a tube of ointment from her cluttered pockets. A glob of greasy goo was applied to each fishy orb, and securing pieces of tape quickly followed. Corneal ulceration thus prevented and her blessing thus bestowed, the fat woman stood aside for the almost-papal procession of gurney, ventilator, IV poles, and ancillary staff that comprises the omnipresent entourage of intensive care patients. Orderlies ran ahead, kicking a path through the packages, tubing, and gauze pads that now littered the floor. Midlin watched them go, sorry to be left alone with his own shameful thoughts regarding his professional performance to date. Fortunately the omnipresent fat woman was there to distract him, producing from amongst a vast sartorial library of pocket books a small paper pamphlet with dog-eared pages and prodding him with it.

"Don't just read this. Memorize it. Live it. Get so you can say it backwards, forwards, sleeping, waking, drunk, sober, and especially under pressure. It changed my life, and you saw for yourself how confident it will make you. I'm Sargent, by the way, this year's chief resident."

"I'm Midlin, I just started today." His face flushed as he realized how unnecessary this comment was.

"Right, I saw your picture. Well, Midlin, next code I see you at I'm having you run, so you'd better get memorizing." And with that she was gone, again astounding Midlin with her rapidity of word and deed.

The pamphlet he now held turned out to be a beacon on this foggy first day. His spirits rose as he scanned the *ACLS*[1] *algorithm* book, for here was the 20-page approach to medicine he had always longed for. Here lay the potential key to recovering his confidence, possibly even to future medical successes. A specific directive or set of directives was given for every life-threatening cardiac rhythm or respiratory emergency, complete with drug dosages and an algorithm tree with clearly marked decision points. His awe of the simplicity and applicability of the directives only grew as he realized the first step of resuscitation was conveniently headed 'A' for airway, and he recalled that airway stabilization had been Sargent's first act on entering the room. The thing was so concise and universally applicable it seemed to make a mockery of the four

[1] Advanced Cardiac Life Support

years he had spent knee-deep in textbooks. He foresaw a rosy future with this book in hand, a future full of efficient and precise resuscitations like the one he had just witnessed and he returned quickly to his padded stool in the corner to begin his initiation. He remained there for some time, raising his feet intermittently for the janitor.

CHAPTER 2

Midlin carefully worked his way up the steps, gripping the handrail with white knuckles. It was July, and so the steps were not icy; the steps were concrete, and so their stability was not in question. He was careful to a fault these days, having now worked a dozen shifts in the emergency room. Danger now lurked everywhere—Midlin was horrified of the things he had seen befall people engaged in seemingly simple tasks and he was determined not to have his entire life change because of a few seconds of inattention. He would never again slice a bagel, separate frozen hamburger patties with a knife, or use a chainsaw and he was considering giving up sex altogether. He had seen a father of three become a quadriplegic while tipping back in his chair, and he had seen a drunk whose car had been struck by a train walk home after kicking off restraints and threatening to shove an "Against Medical Advice" form (with clipboard) up a unit clerk's ass. The random nature of life, death, and grievous injury was thrust before his nose this month, and grandmotherly driving and the wide circumvention of black cats and ladders now characterized his timorous existence.

Despite his growing fear of the world outside Midlin was at least becoming comfortable with the frenetic microcosm of the emergency room. He now felt completely at ease in at least a hundred different medical situations—those hundred for which Sargent had given him lists. She had a list for everything; she knew what to do when your blood pressure dropped, she knew what tests to order when your belly hurt, she knew what questions to ask when you had fevers every night. Her lists had filled Midlin's head to the point of bursting—he actually avoided rapid head movements so as not to jostle them, and he revered like Dead Sea scrolls the paper scraps on which she hastily jotted them. Each time a nurse handed him a chart he felt a brief pang of uncertainty, but then a warm glow of confidence would exude from his brainstem and make his limbs tingle as he mentally sought out the appropriate list without moving his head. To "GI bleeder" he would respond "CBC, coags, type and cross, two large-bore IVs with normal saline running wide open," to "fever" he would answer "CBC, chest x-ray, urinalysis, and blood cultures times two." The words flowed from his lips as if he'd said them two hundred times instead of two, and he always watched for Sargent's approving nod out of the corner of his eye. He had almost forgotten his first day in the emergency room, and apparently so had she.

Midlin scanned the bustling ER hopefully for Sargent's buoyant bulk as he entered, and was relieved to see her animatedly reciting a list near the nurses' station. He then easily spotted Aines, an intern counterpart who Midlin regularly relieved. Aines was obvious in a crowd because of the constant shaking motion of his head, and his enumeration of the many minor tragedies in his life would begin shortly after one was within earshot. He was sitting at a counter in front of a pile of charts as Midlin approached, somehow resting his head on his hand and shaking it at the same time. This time, as it had the last few days, Aines' list of woes began with Sargent. His constant indecision and insecurity tortured her and his lack of organizational skills made it impossible for him to keep up with her breakneck pace. He had, consequently, been a lightning rod for her electrifying discharges of ire.

"She's killing me, been riding my ass all day," he groaned, closing one chart and placing it in a small pile to his left then taking a new one from a tall pile on his right. "I haven't charted a thing, and I'm not going to see the parking lot for an hour." Midlin was about to commiserate but Sargent appeared behind them, called into existence by the mention of her name like the Dark Lord himself.

"Have you seen Hagan's chest x-ray?" She stood over Aines with her hands on her hips, completing his regression to childhood.

"No," he said, in perfect synch with his head shaking.

"How about Smith's CT scan?"

"No," Aines said again, shortly. He clearly had run out of excuses hours ago and now sat before her shaking his head in a pathetic state of learned helplessness.

She looked hard at him, and it clearly didn't take long for her to dismiss him as worthless. She sighed, resigned.

"Sign it all out to Midlin, then, and try to get out of here." The encouraging last phrase clashed with the malevolent look in her eye and Aines gratified her with a cowering flinch. With the distractibility of a puppy she flounced away to attend to a nonspecific bustling in the far corner, and Midlin was left in uneasy camaraderie with Aines. Anxious to prevent the inevitable enumeration of Aines' misfortunes Midlin hurriedly got the necessary patient information, all the while wondering if he would be seeing Aines in the PTSD clinic on his psychiatry rotation. Then as Aines turned back to his charts a nurse approached on Midlin's other side and he was quickly swept up in the bustle of an ER at shift change.

The night progressed as had many others, with Midlin applying his template of organizational lists on the chaos before him. He battled algorithmically with a flood of gastroenteritis and pulmonary edema, all the while mindful of the invisible ogres of clot and ischemia lurking in the background. He was like a machine, processing data and reaching conclusions with such rapidity and certainty that he scared himself. Surely it couldn't be this easy! But always in the corner of his eye was Sargent, flitting in an out of rooms and signing his charts with knowing nods. Her presence assured him that yes, it was possible to think and act this quickly. Here was living proof that her system worked—she strode regally around the emergency room, dispensing judgments never questioned and directives always obeyed. Midlin was envisioning himself as exactly such a presence when his stride was abruptly broken.

The chart said "not feeling well," and Midlin noted incidentally that as with most ER patients this one's vital signs were normal. At first, his discomfort was mild. He simply didn't have a list for this complaint. But some quick questions would resolve that and he expected the workup for fevers, anorexia, nausea, or anemia would soon ensue. What he got instead was a complete collection of war stories, work stories, and romance stories that would keep *Reader's Digest* in material for years. Mr. Larkin had fought in the Battle of the Bulge and had set dynamite charges for the Forest Service, and there had been a story about a mule in a WPA work camp that Midlin simply wished he'd never heard. A full half-hour after Midlin's entrance into the room he stood outside it, leaning against the wall, his head reeling both with the stories he'd heard and the fact that he had acquired no useful information whatsoever. He had no idea how Mr. Larkin didn't feel well, much less why. He didn't know how long there had been a problem, or what had been done already in treating it. The only thing Midlin was certain of was that shortness of breath was not Mr. Larkin's chief complaint.

His eye caught Sargent's from across the room, and he decided immediately to throw himself on her mercy rather than suffer further the verbal onslaught within the room behind him. One thing Midlin already knew was that Sargent was easier on anyone approaching with an appeal to her greatness, and so he advanced meekly with the chart held forth in supplication.

"I need you badly here, Sarg," said Midlin, already seeing the change in Sargent's posture as she prepared to battle either disease or inefficiency (she cared not which). "A real old-timer and a nice guy, but he's just a horrible historian. I know everything about him except what I need."

Sargent looked at the clock and saw that the patient board was light, then grabbed Midlin by the arm and began steering him toward the room. He felt a reluctance to return so quickly to Mr. Larkin's anecdotal assaults but did derive some comfort from Sargent's company, and secretly he wondered if even her military attitude could channel Mr. Larkin's chaotic narration. Mr. Larkin would not be intimidated by her awesome knowledge base or her overbearing presence, and as Midlin himself had learned a friendly approach only brought forth more (and more colorful) recollections from Mr. Larkin. Sargent's confidence as she strode through the door was obvious, but Midlin still couldn't see how she could possibly succeed.

She crossed to the counter and turned to face Mr. Larkin, drawing herself to her full breadth and blurting all in a rush, "Hi Mr. Larkin I'm Dr. Sargent it's nice to meet you Dr Midlin has told me something about you but I need to clarify some things what brings you here this afternoon?"

Deprived of innumerable opening small talk opportunities,

Mr. Larkin sat stunned for a brief moment. But then he rallied, as Midlin knew he would, and offered up a tale of a long-dead cousin who'd left his horse tied up to a...

"OK, Mr. Larkin," Sargent cut in. "I'm here to do a job, and that job is to get as much information as I can in as little time. I can see we're going to have a problem, so let me suggest that you only give me..."

"...o'course who'd a' known the thing would take off like that? Well, there was hell to pay..."

"...ONE WORD ANSWERS!" Sargent's voice, strengthened by countless encounters with otosclerosis[2] (and a diaphragm, Midlin thought, that must be thick as a tabletop), struck Mr. Larkin full in the face and shut him up completely. In that confined space the echoes continued to buffet them all for a few seconds, during which time Sargent regained her composure. Pressing her advantage she started in with questions about fevers, appetite, fatigue and weight loss, each question punctuated by an icy stare that limited Mr. Larkin to a surly "No" each time. Having gained full control of the situation but still with no solid information, Sargent pushed up her sleeves and set her teeth to begin a thorough review of systems. Midlin watched as she actually took her cues from Mr. Larkin's anatomy and asked about each and every one of his bodily parts and functions in turn, beginning with hair and progressing methodically through sight, hearing, smell, taste, swallowing, talking, throat problems (dry? sore? tickling? itching?), and a whole assortment of pains and complaints throughout the body. Mr. Larkin also saw her gaze linger over each anatomic structure in question, as though Sargent were keeping her finger on a list so as not to lose her place, and he made one last attempt at jocularity.

---

[2] The changes in the middle ear apparatus resulting in deafness in many elderly patients.

"Ma'am, when you get to askin' about my privates I hope you won't be starin' like that."

This sentence, of course, petered out in strength throughout its delivery and ended in an uncertain apologetic mumbling in the face of Sargent's stoic visage. Mr. Larkin withdrew like a turtle after that and submitted to the remainder of Sargent's precise history and physical with no further transgressions of protocol. Sargent, on the other hand, seemed to have achieved some sort of blissful state and delivered her questions with her eyelids half-lowered, apparently unaware Mr. Larkin was even in the room. He listed every medication he had ever taken (including detailed questions with regard to over-the-counter laxatives, analgesics, decongestants, and herbal remedies), every surgery he had ever had (additional questioning here revealed an adenoidectomy at age 6), and all known allergic reactions. In response to Sargent's prefabricated social history questionnaire he reported being a widower who lived alone, an ex-smoker, and an infrequent drinker. The fact that questions regarding travel history failed to produce even the hint of an anecdote was also evidence of Mr. Larkin's submission. But when Sargent's canned question "Do you have sex with men, women, or both?" only brought forth a weak "Just women, and one at a time if that's your next question," Midlin knew Mr. Larkin was beaten, for the man could normally have done twenty minutes on that one question alone. The physical exam, with no verbal opportunities whatsoever, seemed to sap him entirely of his remaining energy and at the end Sargent was pulling, pushing, pricking, and hammering away at his utterly lifeless limbs. To Midlin the effect was tragic, like seeing a famous racehorse pulling a coach in Central Park or a once-great athlete in a long distance advertisement. It was with relief that he finally left the room behind. Sargent, feeling in spite of all the recent questioning that he still had no clue as to what was wrong with Mr. Larkin.

Clearly, however, Sargent had her mind made up. She rounded on Midlin abruptly as the door closed behind them with a pointed "Well? What do you want to do?" that took him quite off guard. He had stopped thinking anything at all was wrong with Mr. Larkin half an hour ago and so really had not formulated any plan for dealing with him. His mouth mimicked the stammering in his brain for a minute then finally he rattled off a stock disposition that seemed appropriate.

"Well, we can get a set of basic labs here to be sure there's nothing acutely wrong, then set him up with a clinic doctor and follow-up visits."

The disappointment in her voice and manner told Midlin that this time he had failed to measure up to her high standard of performance. She looked personally hurt as well, and Midlin realized that in his new role as her protégé he would have yet another motivation to excel. It seemed a greater responsibility than he would have volunteered for and he wondered what sublimating equivalent of Aines' head shaking he would develop himself. He hoped it wouldn't be a skin condition.

"Dr. Midlin, you have an elderly patient with a physical complaint who has no caretaker, no primary care physician, and no established diagnosis. Are you telling me you want to return him to his home with no guarantee that he will attend future appointments, follow medication regimens, or ever be accurately diagnosed? Don't you think that hospital admission is appropriate?"

With her perspective on matters phrased like this, of course, Midlin had no choice but to acquiesce with a nod. Everything she had said was true, and even though Midlin had been privy to the same information that she had he had simply not mentally framed it the same way. What he saw was a walking, talking, perfectly functional man with no outward signs of disease or distress whatsoever. What Sargent saw was a complex tangle of social and medical issues too daunting for a simple emergency room evaluation. It was disturbing to him to have assessed the situation so inaccurately, and he was as usual in awe of Sargent's ability to make sense of a seemingly indecipherable morass of information.

Thankfully Sargent did not dwell on this obvious demonstration of his ineptitude and instead turned to a rack of requisition forms on the counter. A stack of papers began to accumulate before Midlin, each triplicate sheet accompanied by a directive from Sargent and each representing untold effort and expense on the part of the hospital staff. She wanted a complete set of blood work including complete blood count, electrolytes, a liver function panel, calcium, magnesium, and phosphate levels, a nutritional evaluation including cholesterol, albumin and prealbumin values, x-rays of the chest and abdomen, an EKG, and various consultation requests including physical therapy, geriatrics and social services. Midlin gathered up his bundle, sought out a patch of empty counter, and plunged in armed with a pen, intent on plowing through this massive sheaf of paper and carbon without further annoying his mentor with gross displays of ignorance. Despite his good intentions he found himself immediately stymied by the first empty blank on the first sheet of paper, and once again he felt his incompetence and indecision manifest as the beginnings of a temporal headache and a layer of prickly sweat soaking his scrubs. He dreaded turning to Sargent again for help, but he didn't see how he could proceed reasonably without filling in the line marked "diagnosis."

His headache worsened and his sweating intensified as he approached Sargent, who upon seeing him at her side asked, "Done already? Good. There's a chest pain in 8 you can see."

Swallowing hard with anxiety Midlin summoned his courage and said, "I'm stuck for a diagnosis, here, Sarg. What should I bill him as?"

Sargent shot a disgusted look past him at the still-blank

stack of papers on the counter, but before the expected tirade came her expression changed. For the first time in their short association Midlin actually waited for her to make a decision, and when it came it was not her usual crisp, authoritative declaration. Instead, there was a series of meaningless utterances until finally a weak "Well…I guess failure to thrive," came forth and showed Midlin that for all her bluster she had no more idea what was wrong with Mr. Larkin than he did. Failure to thrive was no more a diagnosis than "unable to breathe" or "unconscious" and it did nothing whatsoever to guide their future actions. Mr. Larkin might as well have stayed home and watched TV or weeded his garden for all the good they were doing him.

Midlin came out of room 8 in time to see that his order forms had been dismembered into their component yellow, blue, and white sheets and had then been handed to the appropriate nurse, phlebotomist, technician, or patient care aid as well as distributed throughout the hospital in a space-age tube system. Midlin saw the desk clerk hand a final slip to the charge nurse with a smile as she said, "She wants an ESR."

The charge nurse smiled back. "Who's admitting tonight?"

There was now the most definite hint of a twinkle in the clerk's eye and her smile had become more of a smirk. "Too bad, but it's not Flynn. He'd love it."

The two of them were sharing a laugh as Midlin approached, and he pleaded with them to fill him in. "Come on, you guys, I'm new here. What's so funny?"

The charge nurse looked around for Sargent before replying. "Flynn thinks the Erythrocyte Sedimentation Rate is a worthless, expensive test that tells you nothing. He also thinks Sargent is an idiot for ordering them on everyone. It's one of the few things they fight over." Again she and the clerk shared a laugh.

"Well, what do you think?" Midlin asked, wondering what lunatic could stand up to Sargent on a regular basis.

"I think Flynn's a genius," said the charge nurse as she processed the request for the ESR.

CHAPTER 3

Joe was both lucky and unlucky; he was star-crossed yet doubly blessed. He was certainly unfortunate in that he had received a terrible head wound from a baseball bat (though not, as one might think, at the ballpark), but once he hit the ER doors that very wound was his ticket to high-quality, no-waiting medical care. A large man's scalp can be a fatty layer a full inch thick, and such a scalp ripped open will leave a bloody puddle at the victim's feet in under a minute. This sort of wound receives the undivided, even frantic, attentions of all triage nurses resulting in a guaranteed ER bed in seconds flat. Of course an isolated scalp wound is almost never fatal, but even so these patients are whisked through the waiting room past patients with invisible deadly disorders such as myocardial infarction, diverticulitis, and ischemic colitis (conditions indiscernible at first glance from heartburn or gastroenteritis by even the most experienced doctors and never discernable by any faculty at the disposal of a triage nurse). In this respect the stoic patients were at a distinct disadvantage, for even with bloodless presentations the histrionics typical of some types would assure rapid placement as well.

Needless to say Joe, a whooping bleeding Native American, never waited a second in triage. He was rolled quickly into a trauma bay and immediately followed by a press of aides and nurses with an ever more confident Midlin bringing up the rear. There was nothing for him to do in the first minutes as leads, pressure cuffs, pulse oximeter, and IVs and other catheters were placed and the patient was otherwise inaccessible for routine history and physical. At last the hysteria began to subside; the ancillary services done with their respective hose placements and measurements backed away and Joe, apparently calmed by the beeping of his own normal sinus rhythm as well as the near-anesthetic levels of alcohol in his system, slowed his whooping and eventually lapsed into sleep. He lay taped to a flat backboard, and the collar around his neck pushed his fat cheeks upward. Joe's face was red for a variety of reasons, and as Midlin approached he thought it looked like Joe's head might explode.

Midlin began his routine history-taking, starting with his most incisive "What happened to you?" He was still honing his patient interactions in accordance with the model Sargent set, and he had time to pause and appreciate his own delivery. Dispassionate, diaphragm tensed so as to penetrate the alcoholic haze veiling Joe's brain, and straight to the point. She would have been proud. As always, Midlin spent only a few seconds in this self-congratulatory state of mind before it and his dispassionate approach were crushed by Joe's response.

"Some dude hit me with a baseball bat."

The answer struck Midlin briefly dumb, as did the intoxicating vapors emanating from Joe's toothless maw. He knew that all perpetrators in the ER were referred to by the moniker "some dude," and he also knew that the baseball bat was such a common instrument of assault as to have its own chart abbreviation "BBB." What shocked him was this evidence of such ferocious intent to harm and of what a fearsome blow such a tool could deliver. Joe's scalp was hanging from his head like a poorly shellacked balding man's combover, and Midlin's mind jumped immediately to wondering what Joe could possibly have done to deserve such punishment.

"Good Lord! Why would someone hit you on the head with a baseball bat?" The question popped from him reflexively, even though it certainly was not part of Sargent's 11-point History of the Present Illness and it clearly revealed he was not as dispassionate as he had imagined himself moments ago.

Joe opened the one groggy eye that was not swollen shut and regarded Midlin with contempt, then uttered what was (at least to him) the obvious response; "You can't block it."

Midlin, inwardly angry with himself for so obviously demonstrating his naiveté with this question, was at least glad he had not received the stock answer usually given in this situation: "I was standin' on the corner doin' nothin'." This activity more than any other was known to enrage "some dude" and inspire him to acts of extreme violence. Somewhat mollified and trying to recover his place in his history-taking template, Midlin gathered his breath, flexed his abdominal muscles, and bellowed, "How long ago was this?"

But it was to no avail. Clearly the merit of the baseball bat as a weapon was all the information Joe would be imparting that evening. He lay immobile, taped to his board and snoring thunderously. The volume drowned Midlin's loudest offerings and rattled small glass objects on the counters. Even as he marveled at this demonstration of pharyngeal laxity possible only in drunken fat men, Midlin realized his interview with Joe was at an end. After a few half-hearted attempts at traditional techniques such as holding the eyes open, nipple twisting, and toe cracking, Midlin left the room in defeat, having only gleaned information useful to him in future robberies or perhaps revenge killings. As he approached Sargent with his woefully inadequate presentation he knew the problems inherent in this situation: Joe could be bleeding inside his skull from his recent impersonation of a teed baseball or he could simply be drunk as three skunks and thus unable to articulate—there was no good way to sort these out, for even an immeasurably high blood alcohol level did not preclude the former scenario. To make things even worse, Joe could have other injuries he would obviously be unable to describe, especially given his earlier failed attempts to speak his own last name. At the very least Joe would be getting a $700 CT scan of the head to adequately assess whatever irreparable damage had occurred in his most recent misadventure. As for pinpointing further sites of injury, Midlin was absolutely at a loss and innocently wondered if Sargent would request x-rays of Joe's entire body.

It took only seconds for Sargent to see that Midlin knew nothing about his latest charge, but her irritation was short-lived and evaporated when she caught her first glimpse of Joe, whom even a roomful of monitoring equipment couldn't hide from sight. Sargent quickly leapt into action, causing Joe to return both to consciousness and whooping with a well-placed knuckle to his sternum. Next came a series of questions fast enough to confuse Midlin, and while Joe offered up his story in grunts and groans Sargent took each feral noise as an answer based on whether it more closely resembled "yes" or "no." In this expeditious way she rattled off her standard trauma questionnaire and soon was on to the illumination, palpation, percussion and auscultation of Joe's various cavities. Her physical exam in this circumstance was more of a controlled beating and reminded Midlin of the corporal punishment in his

Catholic school. As the nuns had used staplers and rulers to enforce their will Sargent used her stethoscope, reflex hammer, pins and flashlight to push, prod, and poke Joe into a semblance of wakefulness throughout the ordeal. Although the whole performance would make for impressive documentation later (NAI male in no acute distress, Midlin would read. Patient denies fevers, nausea, and vomiting and reports headache with no neck pain, focal numbness, weakness, or incoordination. PERRLA, EOMI, cranial nerves normal and symmetric, lungs clear, heart regular, abdomen nontender, and strength, sensation, and reflexes normal and symmetric) the real truth was Joe had not really answered a question or participated in the examination. He hadn't relaxed when requested, pushed or pulled when pleaded, or breathed when begged. He hadn't imparted any information regarding his exploits (Sargent didn't even know "some dude" was responsible) and he certainly hadn't had a thorough neurological evaluation (Sargent hadn't had him walk on his toes, walk on his heels, or jump on one foot, all of which she considered critical to the accurate assessment of neurological status). Even though Joe was strapped to a board and only semiconscious, Sargent was ready to write her chart note and her orders, selecting the laboratory tests and radiology studies they would need to verify that Joe just needed to sleep it off. She stepped back and began dictating to Midlin, taking her cues as always from the body currently under study.

"Head CT, cervical spine films, thoracic spine films, lumbar spine films, chest x-ray, abdominal series, shoulder films, elbow films, hand films, pelvis and hip films, knee films, ankle films..." Here Sargent paused, and Midlin had just time enough to wonder if she would actually do it before her gaze fell on the marks Midlin had made on Joe's toes. "Foot films," she finished. She had done it. She would x-ray Joe's entire body.

As Midlin took his sheaf of laboratory and radiology request forms (each film and lab test required a separate form for billing purposes) to a nearby counter he watched the activity in Joe's room. First came the weighing team, then the insurance claims representative, then the patient care technicians bearing pillows, blankets and treaded ankle-high socks. All of them encountered the same drunken Joe that he had been and would be for hours and their respective jobs were not as a result made easier. Midlin had time to fill out the required papers for Joe's alcohol level, BUN, creatinine, potassium, sodium, chloride, bicarbonate, calcium, phosphate, magnesium, liver function tests, coagulation times, amylase, lipase, lactate, ESR and toxicology screen before the transportation crew arrived to take Joe to the radiology department for his CT scan and x-rays. A nurse busily began gathering the monitoring equipment and hanging it from the bed as she helped wheel the gurney out the door and Joe's snoring gradually faded down the hallway. A phlebotomist dispatched by Midlin's recent activity scurried after them to procure blood samples before Joe was fully in the clutches of the radiology department. They would be gone over an hour. There would be nothing wrong with Joe, although this would not be reflected in his large, unpaid bill.

CHAPTER 4

As Midlin pulled in to his apartment complex he noted that as usual there was a tan Volvo already parked in the neighboring slot. This was usual in that Tees, the fast-talking, fast-moving owner of that slow-driving beast, was the worst barnstormer Midlin had ever known and typically was home a full half-hour before anyone else in the internship class. Tees would do anything to get out the door quicker, and already had been known to hand over sign-out lists written on cafeteria napkins and to ask fellow interns not only to check the pathology report on a tumor biopsy but also to discuss that result with the patient's family. As his next-door neighbor Midlin knew this more accurately than anyone in the internship class, but he was also more confused by it. Every weeknight he heard Tees' TV faintly through the wall from early news to late news with all the primetime drivel in between, and Tees' seeming preoccupation with getting home for the human interest segment of the local broadcast baffled Midlin. Tees was productive at work and had excellent medical knowledge, so it was at least clear he did something other than sit stupefied on his couch every night while the TV blared.

The one hobby Tees did have that Midlin knew of was women. In this second month of internship the hospital nurses already loved him unconditionally and did his bidding without question, while Midlin couldn't decide if he himself was treated like a child or just an outsider. Tees was a good-looking guy, no doubt, but he certainly was no Redford. In fact, his new long white coat on his long lean frame made him look like a coat rack, Midlin thought. But Tees loved them all; fat or thin, plain or pretty, ambulatory or wheelchair-bound, Tees gave them all that special attention and consideration that brought them under his spell. His gift made his work life much easier, and it had obvious effects on his weekends as well. Midlin had been awakened many Saturday nights to the sound of dance music once Tees had returned home with a selection of the biggest-haired and -breasted offerings of the local establishments.

He entered the building and walked past the sound of Tees' TV, wondering as he did when he would ever live in a house of his own. It seemed yet a lifetime away, like summer vacation viewed from September. Midlin's childhood friends had dropped out of high school and gotten jobs as mechanics, and they had houses. Most of the patients Midlin saw at the hospital had houses, and there was nothing like "4B" or "#29" on the faculty address list. All the same, buried under both undergraduate and medical school loans and making less than $30,000 in his first salaried year, Midlin could not personally imagine ever living without a common wall.

He had only had time to empty his pockets of his keys, pen, stethoscope, reference books, penlight, reflex hammer, and note cards when there was a knock at the door. Tees must have heard him come in. This was the obvious social gesture Midlin had been expecting—they were both working the same ward rotation under Sargent this month and given their proximity they would have to interact at least a little. Midlin had hesitated up until now to make this contact, for with the long hours of inpatient wards and every fourth night call he had not had the strength. He had honestly worried he would fall asleep during one of Tees' enthusiastic tales of womanizing.

"Dinner tonight?" Tees asked when Midlin opened the door. He was in typical form, with his hands and arms flailing wildly. "I've got pasta cooking already, if you don't mind, and afterwards maybe we can play some cards."

Midlin accepted and closed the door with misgivings. He was worried first that someone like Tees couldn't sit still long enough to play cards, and next that if he could they would be up all night. At least Tees' boundless energy had already come into play and Midlin wouldn't have to cook.

Tees' apartment was modern and clean inside, furnished apparently with money from the death of his father (the Volvo, it turned out, was an inappropriate gift from his living mother). Everything was sleek and lean like its owner, from the countertops to the chrome-and-leather furniture to the wall of black electronic components. If he has a dog, Midlin thought, it will be a black-and-silver greyhound that licks itself continuously.

Midlin watched as Tees poured the pasta into a strainer and put it on two plates, then watched with horror as Tees pulled a jar of sauce from the cupboard, opened it and poured it on the pasta. This ancient bachelor tradition had never appealed to Midlin, ancient bachelor though he was. He hated cold coffee, warm fruit, cold pizza and anything else not served as originally intended and this bastardization of the great Italian meal certainly fell into that category.

Tees dropped the plates on the table without mention of a

salad or a vegetable and without asking if Midlin wanted the beer he received. A rapid flurry of forks followed as is typical in meals shared by single men, and they were both done in minutes. Tees leaned back and came as close to relaxing as he could. He tipped back in his chair and looked at ease but his leg jittered constantly and gave him the appearance of a dashboard hula girl. His voice wavered as he talked.

"So, you were in the ER last month? Who'd you work with?"

"Sargent, mostly. Saw a lot of Aines."

"Ouch," Tees winced. "She's almost killed me in 10 days, but now I feel better. So that's how you learned all that shit, huh? Those lists and things? This is your sixth week with her. No wonder you make her so happy."

Tees was smiling when he said this, but Midlin could tell he begrudged Midlin's special treatment at least a little. Midlin was glad to hear mention of his recent efforts at list memorization, and as was his recent habit he breathed silent thanks to Sargent. He blushed a little and questioned Tees in turn.

"Where were you last month?"

"VA, medicine wards. With Flynn most of the time. I lost about 5 pounds, the food there is so bad. And they work it off you, too. No time to memorize any of those lists, that's for sure. But I'll tell you one thing, I laughed a hell of a lot more last month."

Midlin knew what Tees meant. He may have acquired innumerable helpful facts from Sargent, but his last weeks had been decidedly humorless. Flynn, the other chief resident, was a notorious joker who was making work in the otherwise undersupplied, understaffed and undesirable VA hospital across town just bearable. Midlin wasn't scheduled to work with him until after the New Year when Flynn moved to the health palace, and he dreaded the thought of leaving Sargent's comfortable cocoon of knowledge to work with an unknown if popular entity.

"That's too bad you weren't learning, though," said Midlin. "Didn't this guy Flynn teach you anything?" Midlin knew that the real responsibility for medical education lay with the intern or resident himself and not with his various supervisors, but he wanted both to commiserate with Tees and hear more about Flynn. This mysterious figure had been mentioned by almost every member of the residency, but somehow Midlin had yet to meet him. Midlin really couldn't get a good idea of him—people seemed either to hate or worship him, and as Sargent could barely tolerate the mention of his name Midlin had been unable to get any information from her.

"Oh, God, I was learning like you wouldn't believe. It's just that things were a little less, uh, structured."

Tees proceeded to recount the tale of a recent respiratory arrest at the VA. The nurses on the ward had discovered early one morning that Mr. Christman had gone south like a carpetbagger. He had been admitted with a pneumonia and at first had a little trouble breathing, but when his skin turned blue and his pulse and breathing vanished even the VA nurses were alerted to the change in his status. The alarms and squawking pagers had brought the on-call residents and interns running, and the team had begun basic resuscitation measures including placement of an oxygen mask and verification of a running IV. Next the patient was rolled for the placement of a backboard. This was a standard procedure so that the patient's upcoming chest compressions wouldn't simply drive him deeply into the cheap VA mattress. With the patient tipped on an angle Flynn had called a halt to the proceedings and directed attention to the purplish discoloration on the patient's back—a classic appearance of 'livor mortis' and a guarantee that the patient had been dead for at least an hour. In addition the stiffening of the corpse in their hands ('rigor mortis') suggested Mr. Christman might have been dead even longer than that. There was less enthusiasm for the resuscitation following this discovery.

"So Flynn turns to the nurses," continued Tees, "and he says, 'You know how you can figure out how long your VA patient has been dead? Count the food trays in the room and divide by three.' Afterward, Flynn tells me he thinks nurses are just bad babysitters, with a little less diaper-changing and a little more pulse-taking. So, needless to say, I think I learned plenty. Like I said, though, it was a little unstructured."

Midlin spent the remainder of the evening being pummeled in a quirky two-handed variant of spades with which Tees was obviously quite familiar. Tees was buoyed by his victories and Midlin soon realized the chances of his tiring first were remote—Tees appeared just as hyperactive as when Midlin had arrived in spite of a rapid succession of beers. Midlin took advantage of a break in play to plead exhaustion, and as he left Tees predictably turned on his TV to pass a few more hours before bed. Midlin knew that Tees would also have more energy than he in the morning and found the thought slightly irritating.

CHAPTER 5

Mr. Morgan's body was constantly in motion. Either he was wracked by fits of coughing that produced foul, purulent ooze from deep within his lungs or he was shivering from the waves of feverish rigors that washed over him at frequent intervals. He had been an easy one for the ER, and even despite his lack of visible hemorrhage he had passed through triage quickly. A cursory history and physical followed by the chest x-ray that looked exactly as everyone expected was all it had taken for Mr. Morgan to be admitted to Midlin's service with pneumonia. Midlin himself, with almost two months of internship experience, had made the diagnosis from the door by Mr. Morgan's flushed, sweating face and rattling cough.

Mr. Morgan's story, extracted between coughing fits, was typical of his disease. He was a retired business executive who had awakened that morning to the shocking realization that he didn't feel like playing golf. Fevers and a cough had quickly followed the cancellation of his tee time and by late afternoon his breathing had become so labored that he braved the chaos of urgent care. A short three-hour passage from clinic to inpatient ward (a path paved by multicolored paperwork) had been enough for him to develop a slight tachycardia, the first sign of impending septic shock. Midlin had already seen this rapid progression of pneumonia in elderly patients and knew why this disease was previously known as the "old man's friend." Minimal symptoms at bedtime can presage a peaceful death overnight as bacterial products from the lung infection seep into the systemic circulation and cause hypotension, organ damage, and death by virtue of the body's response to them. Mr. Morgan was lucky to have felt sick in the morning.

In spite of his condition Mr. Morgan was surprisingly cheerful, a fact that Midlin had come to see was rare in ill patients. Certainly most sick patients were not as demanding, suspicious, or pernicious as well patients that think they're sick but they could come very close. In addition, Midlin had noted that there was something about shortness of breath that could make a person mean as a snake. Mr. Morgan's bright outlook, therefore, was a particular surprise given his circumstances, and Midlin did his best to minimize the talking and examining so Mr. Morgan could get the rest, hydration and antibiotics he really needed. Midlin knew he was excluding key elements of Sargent's thousand-point admission work-up, but figured the gaps could be filled in the morning when Mr. Morgan was breathing easier. Mr. Morgan was an absolute delight as a patient, for not only was he friendly and grateful but his straightforward presentation and obvious diagnosis meant that Midlin could race through the paperwork and move on to his innumerable other chores. Already tonight he had admitted a cystic fibrotic, a hypercalcemic and an anemic and their presence on the ward made Mr. Morgan's admission seem like a tropical vacation.

Midlin cruised through the admission paperwork, adhering to the age-old mnemonic of ADC VAN DIML:

Admit to internal medicine
Diagnosis pneumonia
Condition stable
Vitals every nursing shift
Activity bed rest with bathroom privileges
Nursing input/output, daily weight
Diet regular
IV normal saline with 20 meq KCl / liter @ 100cc / hr
Medications: Cefuroxime 500mg IV tid
Erythromycin 500mg IV qid
Acetominophen two tablets PO qid PRN
Chloral hydrate 500 mg PO qHS PRN
Phenergan 25 mg PR tid PRN
Labs: CBC, electrolytes, renal panel qd x 3

The words flowed from Midlin's pen without thought as he had already written them a hundred times. It seemed they were always the same no matter what the diagnosis, and it seemed in this case to be a lot of writing just to say "rest, fluid, and antibiotics." To Midlin the rest of it amounted almost to nothing, for he would be in rounds or conference when the weighing team came by to awaken Mr. Morgan at 4 AM or when the nurse dove to catch and record Mr. Morgan's urine before he wasted it in the toilet. Midlin would never see the pathetic regular hospital fare Mr. Morgan would push around on his plate and he certainly wouldn't feel the burning in his veins from continuous potassium infusions and daily needle pokes. Midlin had written these words so often that he had almost forgotten that if Mr. Morgan complained of sleeplessness he would be hit with the chemical equivalent of a sledge hammer (with a similar safety profile) or that if Mr.

Morgan complained of nausea he would be flipped onto his stomach for an even nastier surprise. The untold exertions by innumerable ancillary staff members that Midlin had set in motion were almost immeasurable, and these were simply standard admission orders and Mr. Morgan was simply a standard admission.

Midlin turned next to his admission note, the official documentation of Mr. Morgan's symptoms and physical findings as well as his own plan for correcting them. Here he had some difficulty due to his soft-hearted, abbreviated visit with his patient and he found himself writing larger and leaving wider margins just like he had done in grade school. Although this really didn't compensate for his lack of data it did make for a handsome two pages of documentation, and Midlin had a few seconds to survey it with satisfaction before his pager went off. Sargent was waiting for him in the ER with their latest admission.

On the way out of the ward Midlin came to the penultimate patient door and paused. He drew a deep breath, tucked away loose equipment and clothing, and made a dash for the exit. As always, regardless of the time of day or night, he heard Mr. Larkin's voice follow him down the hall: "Hey, Doc! Have you got a min…"

Mr. Larkin was on his sixth week without a diagnosis. The barrage of laboratory studies had turned up only a mild anemia, and the resultant bone marrow biopsy (after extensive labeled antibody testing) had revealed an infection only seen in dogs. Since that time Mr. Larkin had been x-rayed, CT scanned, ultrasounded, biopsied, endoscoped, and catheterized in every way a very imaginative modern medicine could conceive of without significant diagnostic result. This is not to say there had been no excitement to Mr. Larkin's stay, however, for he had developed bleeding from biopsies, infections from catheters, and perforations from endoscopies with an astonishing regularity. He had been treated with icepacks, blood products, antibiotics and surgeries with no real change in status from his initial presentation. He still didn't feel right and no one knew why.

None of this had affected Mr. Larkin's loquacious manner, and it was obvious now to Midlin that nothing could. Every morning on his requisite rounds Midlin dreaded Mr. Larkin's room for it was a time vortex that took him away from the documentation and meticulous data-gathering that are the essence of internship. Granted he left the room every day with enriching tales of bravery and perversion echoing in his head, but the resultant loss of documentation time had led to many late nights at work and missed dinners with Tees. Mr. Larkin still hadn't warmed to Sargent, though, and her presence was the one defense to his continuous beckonings. Midlin didn't even run past the doorway when Sargent was at his side.

The irony of his running to the ER was not lost on him, and Midlin arrived there ruefully remembering his first day. The sight that greeted him cheered him immensely, for the pancreatitis patient he had come to see was in the Trendelenberg position. This simple maneuver of tilting the gurney to an extreme head-downward angle had been proven not to help in innumerable studies over the past ten years but was still performed by most nurses in most hospitals when a patient's blood pressure plummeted. In this particular instance it meant this simple ward admission for pancreatitis had suddenly become the intensive care unit's problem, for a hypotensive patient would require ventilation, arterial line monitoring, fluid resuscitation, and possibly even pulmonary artery catheterization. As anything beyond an IV was outside the limited resources of both the medicine wards and its nurses these various devices would dictate a stay in the ICU, and there would be that much less paperwork for Midlin that night.

Mr. Owen was a farmer from a nearby rural community who

had decided it was time for Pinky the pig to pay for his room and board. Although Pinky's skull was ultimately crushed in the ensuing scuffle he had managed to land a telling blow just under Mr. Owen's sternum, and the resulting tear in Mr. Owen's pancreatic duct had landed him on his head in the ER. Pancreatitis can arise when the digestive enzymes the pancreas produces begin to digest the pancreas itself, usually because the main pancreatic duct is blocked or torn. The most common causes by far are gallstones in the duct or alcohol use, followed by an extensive list of medications, misfortunes, and maladies that until now had failed to include porcine retaliation. Mr. Owen's pancreatic enzymes were tracking along behind his abdominal cavity, digesting indiscriminately. The resulting inflammation was flooding the area with fluid sucked from his tissues and vessels until there was nothing left for his heart to pump. As Midlin was the ward intern that night and primarily concerned with constipation, sleeplessness, and food quality the vigorous regimen of fluid resuscitation and head-standing Mr. Owen would require was well outside his job description. With a sigh of relief he turned away to tend to more mundane matters but as he did so he caught sight of Sargent on the far side of the room, pestering both the ER resident and the admitting ICU resident with unsolicited advice.

Another feverish sprint past Mr. Larkin's room brought Midlin back to the medicine wards where he was greeted by a sight portending a further reduction in his morning paperwork. Mr. Morgan's symptoms had progressed from intermittent to continuous coughing, and the fluid in his lungs now could be heard gurgling with every breath. This Midlin could hear even over the beeping of the pulse oximeter, whose declining numbers signified a drop in blood oxygen and acted as a countdown for Mr. Morgan's departure for the ICU. Midlin felt first a rush of joy followed by a pang of guilt as he realized that there would be one fewer progress notes to write on his post-call morning. This way of thinking first of workload and next of patient outcome had at first bothered Midlin until he had discovered it was common to all interns. Any given patient may be pleasant, funny, or remind you of your grandmother but once they were on your service they were an added half-hour of paperwork each day. They would need to be interviewed and examined as well as have a chart progress note written, laboratory values checked, and management decisions made at all hours. In addition, each patient lengthened the day in the form of rounds, a daily occurrence in which a literal gang of medical students, interns, residents, fellows and attending physicians examine and discuss each case. A depressed or lonely attending physician could dominate this procedure and prolong it as form of solace, staving off his inevitable return to his dysfunctional family or his empty house. Midlin took some comfort in the fact that he still had not wished for a patient's death in order to avoid daily progress notes (as he knew some fellow interns had), but he was not so strong as to not wish for his own death during some of these marathon sessions.

The attending assigned to ward duty this month was Dr. Cringen, a mousy and balding man who acted as though he were about to adopt, marry, become godson to, or otherwise incorporate into his own family every single patient admitted to the internal medicine service. At the same time that Midlin noted that Mr. Morgan was so short of breath as to be unable to speak he also realized he had failed to ask him all of Dr. Cringen's favorite questions, including those regarding bird ownership and recent travel. Now with this obvious downturn in both their fortunes Midlin clearly was not destined to acquire this information before Mr. Morgan was on the business end of some ventilator tubing, and Midlin dreaded the upcoming confrontation with Sargent and Cringen when they would discover Midlin had failed to determine whether this could be some other-worldly infection or possibly a bizarre occupation-related pneumonitis rather than a commonplace pneumonia. Sargent also had a list of questions to ask her pneumonia patients including recent wool-sorting and mummy-handling that covered all the possible diseases that could masquerade as a commonplace pneumonia, and now that Mr. Morgan was not showing a timely response to the usual antibiotic treatment it looked as if he might be suffering from just such a misdirecting illness. Midlin had mixed feelings as he had Sargent paged, for while he certainly needed her help in intubating Mr. Morgan he dreaded confessing to her his lack of data.

Endotracheal intubation, the placement of a plastic catheter with an inflatable cuff into the patient's airway, is a skill most doctors involved in acute patient care are proficient in. It has been performed since the 1960's, when it came into common usage to aid in the management of injured Vietnam soldiers. Prior to that time, mechanical breathing assistance was only available in the form of the "iron lung" which was used primarily for those with severe polio-related muscular weakness. This contraption sealed at the neck and waist and inflated the lungs by volume expansion—the air in the iron lung would be evacuated, the ribs and chest wall would in turn expand, and the resulting negative pressure in the lungs would cause air to rush (actually crawl) in through the mouth. In that era anyone with respiratory failure due to any cause other than muscular weakness was pretty well done for, for this contraption was unable to overcome the ill effects of fluid within the lung. Placement of a sealed tube in the trachea, in contrast, allows for positive pressure ventilation; a mechanical ventilator is attached to the tube and can deliver pressurized air sufficient to overcome the effects of heart failure or pneumonia.

Midlin prepared to intubate Mr. Morgan with Sargent's intubation mantra running through his mind, "pent, sucs, tube." A traditional, outdated reference to drugs no longer used (sodium pentothol and succinylcholine) but useful in reminding one of the proper sequence of drugs to induce unconsciousness, drugs to cause paralysis, and placement of the endotracheal tube (a curved plastic tube with a stiffening stylet and inflatable cuff at its end) with the aid of a laryngoscope (a wicked-looking curved metal blade for prying open the mouth and lifting the tongue). Midlin tended to all of Sargent's particular details while he waited for her, including testing the cuff inflation and leaving a small syringe attached, tightening the lightbulb on the laryngoscope, pulling the stylet so it no longer protruded beyond the tip of the tube, and placing a rolled towel under Mr. Morgan's head. Each of these maneuvers was specifically engineered to prevent just a few of the potential complications related to intubation, including perforation of the trachea with the stylet and dropping the laryngoscope lightbulb down the trachea to be left to intubate in complete darkness. Such incidents wended their way through the medical literature (sometimes in remarkably obscure and defensive language) to ultimately come to rest in Sargent's many lists, making for apparently quirky behavior in both she and her interns.

His list of chores almost completed, Midlin rifled through the nurses' station drawers in search of an informed consent form. An obvious formality with Mr. Morgan huffing and puffing in his room nearby, such consent did not really exist even when obtained from a patient who was not facing imminent death. The list of complications from any given procedure is far too long to be enumerated in less than a day, and certainly any sane man would turn tail and run upon hearing it. As Midlin wrote the standard potential risks of "infection, structural damage, allergic reaction, and bleeding" he considered how this was at once globally accurate while completely failing to describe the many unsavory potential scenarios. "In performing this procedure I may fracture or dislocate your jaw, knock out any number of your teeth, rupture your esophagus or trachea, drop a small lightbulb down your windpipe, or place the tube in too far thus obstructing a major airway and potentially worsening your condition. Once on the ventilator, lung overinflation can result in an air leak with subsequent life-threatening lung collapse. Your inability to cough and the open passage into the lungs created by the tube will allow additional infections to occur. There have been fatal, unpredictable reactions to all of the medications that will be used for your condition, both in sedating and paralyzing you for placement of the tube and in fighting the infections you have and will have. This will be the first time I will have performed this procedure" would really have been the most accurate depiction of the situation Midlin could produce, but obviously this phrasing was unsuitable.

Mr. Morgan was predictably fatalistic and was grasping for the pen before Midlin had even finished his short, generic list of complications. The whole process was over in less time than it had taken to find the form. With all the necessary preparations made Midlin still felt less than ready and then Sargent fortuitously materialized, at first breathing and sweating heavily. She calmed a bit as Midlin described the situation, and he breathed a sigh of relief when she failed to probe his pathetic database on Mr. Morgan. Midlin was both surprised and mildly pleased to discover that her supervision of his first intubation was an actual relaxation for her. Aines was the other ward intern tonight, and by comparison Midlin was Galen[3] himself. The few decisions that Aines had ventured to make this year had been disastrous, and so recently he had progressed from agonizing indecision to an absolutely decisionless state. He had in recent evenings stood fidgeting above arrhythmias, septic and hemorrhagic shock, strokes, and

---

[3] Often considered the father of medical investigation, like most ancients Galen actually was never correct.

one patient who admittedly not even the autopsy could diagnose. Sargent had shown impressive endurance in dealing with Aines, both in the diligence of her supervision and in the incessant verbal abuse she heaped upon him. A moment of peaceful intubation requiring only adherence to a list was apparently what she needed to relax.

Sargent surveyed Midlin's preparations and gave him a final nod to proceed. The red "code cart" seal had been broken (a singular act adding several hundred dollars to Mr. Morgan's bill) and Midlin grasped one of the premixed medication syringes labeled "etomidate." Although he had witnessed it numerous times before, Midlin was again surprised that Mr. Morgan's eyelids began to droop before the entire contents of the syringe could be injected into his intravenous line. This phenomenon had caused Sargent to affectionately murmur the phrase "direct physiologic control" on more than one occasion in the past with reference to the intravenous line, and Midlin now felt a similar rush of confidence as Mr. Morgan drifted into unconsciousness. He noted with relief that the heart rate and blood pressure monitors never changed in their beeping and tracing; hypotension (a drop in blood pressure) was a common problem with the older induction agents such as sodium pentothal but was now mercifully uncommon with the newer medication options. One thing that hadn't changed, Midlin thought wryly, was that both pharmacists and doctors still had no idea how these drugs worked. He moved on to the syringe of vecuronium.

Muscle paralytics had also come a long way in recent years. The older drugs such as succinylcholine had caused dangerous metabolic abnormalities as well as a bizarre twitching following their administration. Under the influence of a second-generation paralytic, however, Mr. Morgan became slack without grotesque and undignified jerking. Midlin paused briefly to consider Mr. Morgan's unconscious, paralyzed form but with the realization that his next breath had to be through an endotracheal tube Midlin grabbed frantically for the laryngoscope. A typical patient will show a drop in blood oxygen within one minute, and so Midlin had only that long to pry open the jaw and lift the tongue with the laryngoscope, view the vocal cords, pass the stylet-stiffened tube past them into the trachea, inflate the terminal cuff of the tube, and hook the tube to a squeezable bag for ventilation. The trachea is inconveniently located for this procedure, lying far in the front of the neck and guarded at its opening by both the vocal cords and the epiglottis, a flap of tissue that caps the larynx and guides swallowed material into the esophagus. The design is such that endotracheal tubes as well as food pass by the trachea and end up in the stomach, where the effect on blood oxygenation is minimal.

Midlin opened Mr. Morgan's lifeless jaws, a feat made easy by his paralyzed state. In spite of unconsciousness most reflexes remain intact and patients writhe, gag, and even vomit without the use of vecuronium. Midlin guided the curved blade of the laryngoscope into the mouth, levered the tongue forward, and looked hopefully down Mr. Morgan's gullet for a sight of the vocal cords. There was nothing but wet pink tissue to be seen. Midlin gulped with anxiety and tried to mentally gauge how much time had passed since Mr. Morgan's last ineffectual breath. Fifteen seconds? Thirty seconds? He hated to quit so quickly but time was running short while he flailed around in Mr. Morgan's hypopharynx. As he craned his neck around to ask for Sargent's help he felt her hand grab the laryngoscope over his. Her whole body stiffened as she lifted the tool up and away instead of making the prying motion Midlin had been ineptly attempting. Midlin's heart raced as the tongue, jaw, tissues and epiglottis all shifted forward and the vocal cords came into view. Before the glorious sight disappeared Midlin shoved the tube forward and saw it spread apart the cords and enter the trachea. He was not able to revel in the moment, however, for a newly arrived respiratory therapist shoved him aside, taped the tube in place, attached it to a rubber bag, and began squeezing. Stethoscopes were produced from every pocket in the room and were applied to Mr. Morgan's chest as listeners strained to hear the telltale sounds of air entering each lung with equal force. A tube placed too far into the trachea will block one main bronchus and overinflate the other, a situation that could hardly be of help to Mr. Morgan. Midlin was pressed to the wall by the massive portable x-ray machine which had arrived to verify the position of the tube by its metallic marker, and in spite of Sargent's supervision and the satisfied expressions of those with stethoscopes he still was nervous about the result. A lung obstructed by improper tube placement would go from air-black to liquid-white quickly as the air beyond the obstruction is absorbed by the bloodstream, and the twenty minutes it would take to develop the x-ray could then be Mr. Morgan's last given his already poor lung function.

Midlin began to relax as the x-ray machine made way for the mechanical ventilator and the pulse oximeter, reading the amount of hemoglobin-bound oxygen by light beams in Mr. Morgan's fingertip, stayed at a steady 99%. The pressurized air and pure oxygen provided by the ventilator would keep Mr. Morgan alive until the antibiotics could gain the upper hand on his unwelcome bacterial visitors. He was off to the ICU, where plastic tubes would breathe, eat, drink, urinate, and defecate for him in the interval, and the ubiquitous parade of phlebotomists, EKG technicians, charge nurses and insurance representatives arrived to ease his passage. Midlin's presence in the room was clearly no longer justified, and he followed Sargent out to the nurses' station.

The ICU intern this month was Tees, and he had been summoned to supervise Mr. Morgan's transfer. He stood fidgeting over Mr. Morgan's thin chart, as always looking anxious to move on to his next task. He looked up as they approached and proved that he had already read Midlin's paltry, insufficient admission note.

"Lobar pneumonia, huh? Probably hasn't been on the juice long enough. We'll get him through it," he said, gathering up documents. Ever since his association with Flynn last month he had been less inclined to discourse and more to action, and without further discussion of the situation and somewhat in violation of academic protocol he was gone. His abrupt departure allowed him to avoid the exhaustive enumeration of differential possibilities with which Sargent was bursting, and so she turned her attention to Midlin.

"Has Mr. Morgan ever worked as a museum curator or loom operator?" she asked.

CHAPTER 6

Midlin joined the flow of traffic into the conference room, cradling his lunch in his arms and wishing he'd waited to open his soda until he was seated. He was jostled on all sides by white coats, all of which were worn by superiors unlikely to appreciate a brown blemish for the duration of the upcoming afternoon. He was a finicky eater and did not relish the thought of this monthly lap lunch, but it was hard enough to escape his clinical duties for this hour without trying to grab a quick bite afterward. Clinical mishaps and their attendant pages had actually precluded his attendance at a complete conference so far this year, and he hadn't even gone so far as to arrange a page from a friendly nurse at 12:05 as he knew Tees always did. As he entered the conference room with the last of the attendees he noted as always that nothing had changed since elementary school and the only available seats were in the front rows. The effect was such that Aines, standing behind the podium and prepared to present the day's case, appeared to be suffering from halitosis or some other pungent malady.

The mortality and morbidity conference is a cornerstone of medical education. Each month a resident presented the particulars of a case that had gone sadly awry, resulting in the death or permanent disability of a patient. Although such occurrences were commonplace enough in the course of a normal illness, the cases chosen for these conferences involved an initial misdiagnosis, procedural complication, inappropriate treatment, or some other avoidable iatrogenic blunder. The resident assigned to present the case culled the many available charts, lab values, pathology specimens and radiographic studies pertinent to the case and stood before the assembled intellectual might of the hospital for a detailed criticism of his thought processes and actions. The simple acts of creating overhead transparencies, researching relevant medical literature, recruiting specialist testimony, and acquiring the important but elusive pathology slides and radiographs were enough to test the limits of even an efficient resident like Tees. Aines, demonstrating no such organizational skills, had shown an expected evolution from head shaking to corporeal shuddering on the few occasions he had been sighted over the last month. Midlin fervently hoped not to witness a pathetic and public decompensation, even though his dollar had bought the 12:45-12:50 slot in the residents' betting pool.

Midlin had just had time to balance his lunch on his knees and set his drink on the floor when the conference mediator, Dr. Rossen, began his introduction. He strode back and forth demonstrating his typical pomposity as he set the stage for Aines, his confidence and precision impressive enough to attract any number of female medical students despite his garish wedding ring. Most residents who had presented at this conference were less impressed with Dr. Rossen's diagnostic acumen as they knew he insisted on a thorough review of all materials prior to the assembly. Much like Alex Trebec pretending to know the answers to all questions on *Jeopardy*, Dr. Rossen would occasionally offer up diagnostic suggestions that were invariably accurate and insightful yet surprised very few attendees. His predictive abilities would be insufficient, however, to foresee and avoid his *in delicto* disclosure in a broom closet later in the year. He at last yielded the floor to Aines with a final preening gesture and flourish.

Aines' presentation began with the same stock phrase that initiated all such conferences, "the patient was seen initially in the walk-in clinic with a cough." Every retropharyngeal abscess begins as a sore throat, many leukemias initially manifest as head colds, and a brain tumor often presents as a headache. This walk-in clinic is the hospital's great generic patient intake, where 99% of patients are perfectly healthy and 100% of them are treated as though they are. Obviously every patient can't be given a neck x-ray, bone marrow biopsy, or head CT scan and so they are all treated with antibiotics, decongestants and aspirin. This system of investigating returning patients more thoroughly and thus weeding out the worried well is a basic principle in medicine and rarely results in lasting harm to the patient. Unfortunately, at every mortality and morbidity conference the awareness of this fact is suspended (as it always is by the general public) and the clinic is implicated as the first of many mistakes contributing to the patient's demise.

Allowing the knowing nods and murmurs to die down following mention of the beleaguered walk-in clinic, Aines proceeded to relate the unfortunate tale of Mr. Gabelli. His initial treatment with antibiotics and cough syrup having been ineffectual, he had returned for a second visit. The subsequent chest x-ray showed a "spot" rather than the expected pneumonia, and Mr. Gabelli began his slide on the slippery precipice of patient care. Such nodules are common findings and can denote anything from a life-ending cancer to a scar from a twenty-year-old tuberculosis infection. As with many such "spots" the underlying cause was not immediately apparent, and the subsequent studies of Mr. Gabelli's sputum and blood also predictably yielded no diagnosis. He therefore underwent bronchoscopy, in which a flexible fiberoptic scope was snaked down his anesthetized airway and samples of the cells lining his bronchi were obtained by saline washing and brushing. It was these folded, mangled, matted cells that landed on the pathologist's microscope stage and sealed Mr. Gabelli's fate.

The analysis of 'cytology' specimens can be fraught with difficulty. The cells under investigation have been removed from their normal surroundings and have undergone considerable mutilation in their harvesting. Even the most basic distinctions can be difficult in this setting, and furthermore their interpretation can vary markedly from one pathologist to another depending on the experience and even the mood of the interpreting physician. Too few or too many cups of coffee that morning, a frustrating home life or financial situation, or even a recent article or conference emphasizing previously unappreciated cellular characteristics can all affect the ultimate diagnosis. In the case of Mr. Gabelli the caffeinated, overeducated pathologist was certain he saw the effects of the *Mycobacterium tuberculosis* bacterium in the bronchial cells and accordingly unleashed the might of the hospital's microbiologists and infection control specialists. Mr. Gabelli was placed on three specialized antituberculous antibiotics, remaining samples from his bronchoscopy were set aside for prolonged culture incubation, and the infection control teams assessed his home environment and provided his family members with prophylactic medications. The fact that his notoriously unreliable tuberculous skin test was negative bothered no one. Similarly, the absence of any characteristic red-staining bacteria was unconcerning, for a tuberculosis

infection can involve a remarkably small number of organisms and incubated cultures can take weeks to produce the offending agents.

In the ensuing year of treatment for his tuberculosis Mr. Gabelli returned repeatedly to the clinics for laboratory tests evaluating his liver (which can be damaged by the antituberculous medications), for prescription refills, and for empty reassurance with regard to his continued coughing. The treatment of tuberculosis often requires a full year of medication and so his insistence that he was not improving fell on deaf ears, most notably those of Aines. Aines, having inherited the case halfway through from a departing resident, had the words of the excitable pathologist echoing in his head and he was unable to ignore or even be suspicious of them. Only when the course of medication was complete and he was declared cured could Mr. Gabelli finally coax Aines into his familiar state of doubt, and a repeat chest x-ray was ordered at last.

Here there was a pause in the presentation as the chest x-ray was produced from a large stack of films and placed on the overhead projector. Of course simply his selection as a topic for this conference implied that Mr. Gabelli's story would be tragic, but even this knowledge was insufficient to prepare the crowd for the sight they beheld. There was now a lump of tissue roughly the size of a grapefruit in Mr. Gabelli's right lung. CT scan films followed and showed bones, a liver, and a brain that all resembled Swiss cheese in the classic pattern of metastatic small cell lung carcinoma. Each successive film sheet drew more groans and sighs from the crowd, for the truth was apparent even to doctors unaccustomed to interpreting these complex images. Mr. Gabelli was absolutely riddled with cancer.

The subsequent discussion followed the typical course of a mortality and morbidity conference. The pulmonologists who had procured and the pathologists who had interpreted the cytology specimens defended their accuracy, and one pulmonologist actually suggested that Mr. Gabelli had cancer *and* tuberculosis. Next came the infectious disease department's justification of their treatment of Mr. Gabelli in the absence of laboratory, culture, or skin test abnormalities, which one doctor claimed he would do again should a similar situation arise. Lastly, the oncology department representatives exonerated themselves with the simple statement that they had never been consulted on the case. One humbling statement from a medical student in the front row to the effect that a direct biopsy of the lesion would have averted this disaster was accepted with a brief, introspective silence. The implied but unstated undercurrent to the entire discussion was, of course, that Aines was to blame for the whole fiasco simply because he was behind the podium.

The clock now read 12:51, and as statements of individual defense and communal commiseration wound down Midlin kissed his dollar goodbye. Aines had held up reasonably well, his continuous head shaking being variably interpreted as admission of guilt, sorrow at his patient's circumstances, and even a nervous tic portending psychiatric illness. In a voice shaking in time with his head, Aines turned the topic of conversation to the treatment of Mr. Gabelli's *corpus caseus*[4], which by now most likely contained proportionately more tumor by weight than normal cells.

The suggestions for Mr. Gabelli's management were as varied as the personalities and specialties in the room. The radiation oncologists wanted to irradiate his brain and spinal cord. The hematologists wanted to biopsy his bone marrow while the gastroenterologists wanted to biopsy his liver. Dr.

---

[4] Literally, "cheese body." Not an accepted medical use of Latin.

Cringen wanted to meet with the patient's family to discuss the social implications of the situation. The hospital's legal representation wanted Mr. Gabelli to sign a tall stack of forms. Everyone could guess that the surgeons would want to cut out the biggest piece, although as always there were no surgeons present at this academic conference. The oncologists, receiving the most general support, wanted to begin Mr. Gabelli's chemotherapy. Given the extensive spread of the cancer this was the most reasonable option since measures such as surgery and radiation therapy could only treat a limited focus of disease.

Here the discussion faltered somewhat. The question before the oncologists was: which chemotherapy regimen to administer? What exact dose and combination of the available forms of intravenous battery acid, each of which individually has been shown to slightly decrease the growth rate of some cancers, should be utilized? What exact chemical means should be used to create the familiar absence of bone marrow and blood cells, the sloughing of mucous membranes, and the ensuing widespread bleeding and infections? What adjunctive steps with surgery and radiation therapy should be taken, if any? These conundra generally could not be solved in a conference setting of this sort, for the answers lay within the national tumor registry databanks and available research studies sponsored by the National Institute of Health. Current research projects had to be surveyed and cross-referenced with Mr. Gabelli's pathology results, and only then could a combination regimen with a catchy acronym like CHOP or MOPP be selected. No normal human could possibly carry this vast amount of information in his head, and so all present were willing to defer this discussion pending further data acquisition. Things seemed to be winding down as Dr. Rosser acknowledged Sargent's raised hand.

Sargent stood and began outlining the situation in a precise, algorithmic fashion. She cited all the potential expected tumor subtypes and the corresponding treatment acronyms currently under study in national trials. She laid out the possibilities in succinct, organized statements that reduced the situation to a rational navigation of the labyrinthine possibilities, and in doing so clearly revealed a vast, current body of knowledge that was remarkable. While Midlin sat proudly by and reveled in the fact that he was considered her protégé, he did suffer some inward misgivings. She detailed the various chemotherapy regimens in such a detached manner and with such cold objectivity that it was clear to Midlin that she was not visualizing the horrific effects of these treatments on Mr. Gabelli in any way. She was imagining a calendar of office visits, hospital admissions, and drug administrations without so much as a thought for the attendant pain, suffering, inanition, cost and loss of dignity and autonomy that Mr. Gabelli would endure as a result. Midlin's mind ranged through the scenario as Sargent summed up her recitation, at first sincerely wondering what he would opt to do if in Mr. Gabelli's position and then surprised to discover himself envisioning a variety of tropical cruises in succession rather than the brand of extravagant expenditure Sargent was pedaling.

Midlin was awakened from his dreams of terminal sun tanning by Dr. Rosser's closing comments. "Thank you for your contributions, Dr. Sargent," he said, clearly as awed as the rest of the room at Sargent's impressive knowledge. "Does anyone have any additional suggestions for Mr. Gabelli's care?" he asked, and at first Midlin thought the laughter that ensued was due to the impossibility of adding to Sargent's analysis. He quickly realized, however, that the laughter was spreading outward from the back corner of the room like ripples in a pond. Midlin's eyes fixed on the apparent source of the disruptive comment even as Dr. Rosser addressed him, and as he regarded the mischievous light in the bright eyes of this blond Irish imp he knew with certainty that at last he was looking at Flynn.

Dr. Rosser's attitude indicated that he knew generally what to expect, but he clenched his jaw and made the necessary confrontation. "Dr. Flynn, do you have a suggestion for Mr. Gabelli's future management?"

Flynn waited until every member of the crowd had turned and could fully appreciate his grin. "I'd have him take up skydiving," he said. Then as an afterthought he added, "Aines may as well go, too."

CHAPTER 7

The walk-in clinic waiting room was absolutely packed. This was usually the case, as most patients are not lucky enough to wake up with an illness on the day of a doctor's appointment. People were standing along the walls, sitting on the floor, and haranguing the triage nurse and Midlin felt he could actually see the pall of infectious droplets hanging in the air as he walked by. Those who weren't sneezing and coughing as a result of this year's rhinovirus strain soon would be after the typical four-day incubation period. Those who were coughing and sneezing most likely had rhinovirus colds, but every so often one such patient would return to become the topic of the next mortality and morbidity conference. Midlin had some small solace in the thought that at least this wasn't the pediatric clinic where the screaming, commotion, and infectious droplet pall were trebled and where the free baby formula and toys provided by the hospital assured the constant attendance of the fecund lower classes. Even so, Midlin considered all clinics torture, with limited time and resources and excessive patient load. He had heard Flynn quoted as saying the internship year consisted of "six months of inpatient wards, two months of ER, one month of ICU, one month of subspecialty training, and five years of clinic."

Midlin spotted the thin chart on the top of the stack at the same time he saw Tees rapidly moving in from the far side of the room. This one was gorgeous, clearly a chart belonging to a new, uncomplicated patient or perhaps even a young, healthy, clean, intelligent and intelligible professional with a cold. A chart like that required no extensive review—there would be no prior EKGs to compare, no previous hospital admissions to peruse, and no lengthy medical history to absorb. Even as he broke into a sprint Midlin doubted his chances, for Tees moved faster than most and was already on the move. Midlin was bigger, though, and managed to block Tees out at the last second as if they were in the lane. Rather than a rebound, Midlin was able to pluck the insubstantial manila folder from the top of the stack and step aside, leaving for Tees a thick disorganized beauty with the dreaded words "3rd chart of 3" stamped on its face. Tees would be busy an hour at least. In good faith each intern had to take the next available chart, but short of this patient assignment ranked with love and war.

Mr. Escobar was visiting from out of state and had not brought enough insulin for the trip. He was a portly man in his sixties, and so clearly had the adult-onset type of diabetes. This disorder results from a reduced tissue response to insulin ("insulin resistance") that has its roots both in genetics and obesity, and results in higher insulin levels than normal. This is in marked contrast with juvenile-onset diabetes, in which the immune system itself destroys the pancreatic islets of Langerhans responsible for insulin production and there is a resultant absence of the precious hormone. Although these disorders are not as age-specific as the names would imply, most juvenile-onset diabetes strikes younger patients and on the rare occasions such patients live to Mr. Escobar's age they are easy to identify by their amputations, blindness, and coronary and carotid artery surgery scars. The combination of high blood sugars and administered insulin causes a rapidly progressive atherosclerosis with the resultant vascular complications such as heart attack, stroke, renal failure, claudication[5], and peripheral gangrene. In addition, the elevated blood glucose inhibits the function of the immune system and puts the juvenile diabetic at risk for overwhelming infections. The nerves also respond poorly to marination in sugar water, and many diabetics eventually develop burning, pain and numbness in their lower extremities. Mr. Escobar, in contrast, was controlled for many years on pills alone and only recently had been placed on insulin. His insulin dosage would now increase along with his weight and years in an attempt to overcome his growing insulin resistance until eventually he would develop the same vascular, infectious, and neurologic complications. This would occur over the course of fifteen years or more compared to the much more rapid progression of juvenile-onset complications.

Even though Mr. Escobar had shown little ability in the realms of mathematics and planning, he was certainly otherwise a meticulous patient. Insulin is released from the pancreatic islets in response to a meal, and it allows the sugars digested and absorbed into the bloodstream to be taken up and used by the cells of the body. The diabetic patient theoretically should check his blood sugar level four times a day (a standard rarely met) when first determining or adjusting his insulin dose and learn to balance the size and sugar content of his meal with the

---

[5] From the Latin, claudio, "to limp." Used to describe pain with walking due to insufficient blood flow.

size of his insulin injection. Too little insulin and the blood sugar remained high, unavailable to the body's tissues (giving rise to the poetic description "starvation amidst plenty") and bathing the cells with sugar and subsequent complications. Too much insulin and the voracious uptake of glucose causes blood sugar levels to plummet and the state of "insulin shock" results, with its attendant risks of seizure and death. Such a state can also be precipitated by vigorous exercise as muscle cells can utilize glucose without the stimulus of insulin, and this effect in moderation can go a long way in reducing the medication needs of many diabetics. Mr. Escobar had dutifully recorded the size of every meal and insulin dose with the subsequent blood sugar reading every day for the last several months, and carried a stylish kit including glucometer, syringes, finger lancets, and test strips as well as his blood sugar diary. Midlin noticed that the compartment for insulin was empty, however, a fact that rendered all this careful documentation useless.

To wait for insulin a week or two until his return home would most likely have no discernable ill effects on Mr. Escobar. His sugar would run relatively high (with readings of 200 or 300 rather than the normal 100) and the gradual deterioration of his tissues would be slightly hastened during that time, like the effects of a long skid on the life of a tire. The classic hyperglycemia symptoms of blurred vision and excessive thirst and urination (polydipsia and polyuria) rarely develop under glucose levels of 300, and such levels are rarely seen in adult-onset diabetics under at least some form of treatment. The symptoms result from the loss of sugar in the urine at levels over 300, and this phenomenon is the origin of the full name diabetes mellitus or "sweet urine." The juvenile-onset diabetic, in contrast, could develop these symptoms as well as the life-threatening "diabetic coma" or ketoacidosis in just 24 hours of insulin deprivation. The resultant metabolic derangement would result in the formation of ketones and a fruity smell on the breath, giving rise both to the name of the condition and to an unusual sniffing behavior in older doctors (the urine-sipping doctors of the previous generation having mostly died out). In spite of this relative lack of risk, a patient with such an established routine as Mr. Escobar could hardly be denied. Midlin was gratified that at least, unlike so many others, Mr. Escobar knew his exact dose and type of insulin.

The discovery of insulin in the 1920's was revolutionary in many ways. It represented the first successful isolation of a hormone and allowed for treatment preparations of pig and cow pancreas to be made and administered. These preparations were problematic, however, and the presence of foreign pork and beef proteins caused immune reactions as well as unpredictable dosing. The modern diabetic suffers none of these complications as all current commercial preparations contain only human insulin in different strengths and vehicles to allow variable durations of action. Rather than by smashing human pancreas, however, this human insulin is produced by vats of the friendly gut bacterium *Escherechia coli* that have been inoculated with the human gene for insulin. These primitive, one-celled organisms are as phylogenetically far from human as any can be, and yet their enzymatic machinery is able to read and translate the human DNA as well as produce a perfect human insulin molecule (a feat that had frustrated all test-tube attempts). Most anthropologists are in agreement that there is no real "missing link," that actually our anthropologic data is most convincing. In spite of this, the provision of such a catch phrase to the suggestible opponents of evolution has resulted in its continued utterance in spite of its inaccuracy. In fact the point is moot—the millions of diabetics today are living proof that not only did man descend from apes, he descended from bacteria.

Mr. Escobar's case could not have been more straightforward. Although a simple prescription for insulin was all that was required, Midlin was still obligated to present the patient encounter to Sargent for approval. Sargent was in charge of the clinic that day, supervising a number of interns and nurse practitioners and consequently running from room to room in her usual state of frantic energy. She was responsible for everything that went on in the clinic that afternoon, and she would hear presentation on and meet every patient seen that day. She reveled in this role, dispensing wisdom and demonstrating techniques to her various underlings and describing each great discovery as a medical "classic." Sargent saw textbook cases everywhere she looked and constantly cited "classic" triads of presentation, examination findings, and laboratory values to her surrounding subordinates. The concepts she discussed were usually just within Midlin's understanding given his previous eight years of science classes and medical training, although certainly most of the singular facts she enumerated were new to him. The nurse practitioners, however, benefiting from only one-fourth the medical education, were completely unable to understand Sargent's statements or meet her performance standards. Sargent was unable and unwilling to conceal her contempt for the nurses, and as a result most of them hated her and all of them feared her.

Given that the day was so busy there was quite a line forming at Sargent. She listened to each fledgling caregiver describe his respective case, berated him for his inaccurate conclusions, and expressed disgust for his omissions. Then, with an unmistakable "If you want something done right…" expression on her face she would lead the way into the patient's room to duplicate all the work just performed and alter completely the diagnoses and treatment plans recently rendered by the intern or nurse practitioner. On such days most of the trainees would tag along into the various patient rooms, partly to receive the additional knowledge but also to see others suffer

Sargent's intellectual terrorism. They were especially pleased to see that Midlin was not spared.

"Exam findings?" she asked, following Midlin's description of Mr. Escobar's insulin quandary.

With fearful dread Midlin realized that given the circumstances he hadn't really examined Mr. Escobar. He hadn't and still didn't see the point of performing Sargent's 100-point physical exam on a man with such a simple request, and he fell back on a simple statement he knew would be true, "Well, his heart and lungs are clear."

Sargent groaned as if Midlin were a nurse practitioner. "You didn't check for evidence of retinopathy, neuropathy, or vascular insufficiency? Did you even plan to check basic laboratory tests and an EKG?"

"Well, no," answered Midlin. "He is clearly under another doctor's care, and all of that didn't seem necessary. Certainly that's all being done at his regular clinic visits."

"You are placing a lot of faith in a doctor and a clinic you don't know," Sargent responded. "If my name is going on this chart and insulin prescription we have to establish this patient's adequacy of glucose control and screen him for complications."

With this, she led her trainee entourage into the room.

Mr. Escobar, like most patients, was a little surprised at the massive influx of white coats into his tiny room. Most patients didn't realize the difference between private hospitals and teaching facilities and were shocked to see their personal and confidential medical information paraded before a whole contingent of medical trainees. Mr. Escobar recovered well, however, and began answering Sargent's rapid-fire questions with regard to his eating habits, insulin dosage, urine output, and foot care. Sargent's gaze was drawn to Mr. Escobar's socks and shoes which clearly precluded examination of his feet.

"This is something I never want to see from any of you again," she said, addressing the room. "No diabetic should be seen in a clinic room with socks and shoes on." She looked pointedly at Midlin as she continued, "We have no idea if this patient is developing neuropathy, vascular insufficiency, or ulcers." She began removing the offending coverings with unnecessary violence to further make her point, and then perused the exposed appendages with excessive care.

"As we all know, the diabetic's foot is prone to ulceration with delayed healing. This is due to a combination of poor vascular supply and reduced immune response and can develop in the space of one day, often without pain due to poor nerve function. Just one wrinkle in the sock or a stubbed toe can dramatically change the next years of a diabetic's life. Early detection and appropriate local care are therefore critical." Sargent, typical of many academic doctors, spoke as if Mr. Escobar and the foot in question were not even in the room with them.

Sargent then led them on a thorough examination of Mr. Escobar's entire body, specifically directing their attention to areas potentially affected by diabetes. She darkened the room and inspected the retinas with an ophthalmoscope—a feat performed rarely and poorly in the clinic and one which Midlin had never really mastered. The definitive evaluation of the retina could only be performed by an ophthalmologist with a slit lamp device following pharmacologic dilation of the pupil, and Midlin knew exactly what he would see with the pocket ophthalmoscope even as he took his turn in the darkened room. He suffered through the usual views of solid black, glaring white, and then a fuzzy pink color that he made a brave show of bringing into focus with clicks of the lens dial. Upon his stepping back he heard Sargent declare she had seen the signs of "classic" early neovascularization—the proliferation of blood vessels in the retina that would eventually obscure Mr. Escobar's vision to the point of blindness if untreated. Midlin could see by the looks of the others in the room that their experiences had been similar to his, and that no one else had appreciated the ingrowth of tiny new blood vessels on the inner lining of Mr. Escobar's eyes.

Sargent next listened in turn to the patient's carotid, renal, and femoral vessels to detect a 'bruit'—the gurgling of blood resulting from turbulent flow in atherosclerotic arteries. She did this while attempting to disregard the superimposed sounds of breathing, digestion, and flatulence that obscure most of the useful information, a feat Midlin had always found difficult at best. In addition, this exam presumed many other facts including normal cardiac valve function, normal hydration status, and normal vascular smooth muscle tone. With these confounding elements the findings can be elusive, deceptive, or prone to misinterpretation. This feat accomplished, she moved on to Mr. Escobar's heart and lungs. This portion of the exam is as fraught with difficulty as any, and Sargent braved the misleading effects of hydration, heart rate, and breathing which can make a heart murmur appear or vanish seemingly at random. Her initial lung examination resulted in a furrowed brow and most likely revealed sounds suggesting pneumonia, but after she asked her subject to cough hard and breath deeply the sounds apparently disappeared and she herself breathed easier. The partially collapsed lungs of a sedentary patient can perfectly mimic a life-threatening pneumonia, and conversely a life-threatening pneumonia can make no sound at all.

Sargent then returned to Mr. Escobar's feet for the neurologic examination. This consisted of extensive prodding with a procession of pins, blunt probes, and tuning forks followed by a seemingly ridiculous sequence of toe wiggling and strength testing. The variety of testing procedures corresponded to the variety of nerve fiber types, each of which could be affected independently by diabetes. There were nerves for pain sensation, vibration and position sensation, and motor function and the exam was intended to evaluate each type. Mr.

Escobar patiently succumbed and was deemed neurologically sound, being able to sense with his eyes closed both which direction his toe had been moved and with which instrument he had been assaulted. He was mercifully spared walking like a duck and a ballerina given the cramped quarters in the small clinic room.

As her final act Sargent polled the attendant trainees on the appropriate routine laboratory testing for a diabetic, and following a glare from her Midlin began to record the suggestions on laboratory order forms. Tees, at last joining them and ready to present the results of his afternoon of chart review, listed most of the recommended tests while Aines managed to blurt out "EKG" and then looked at the floor and chewed his lip, a new one for him. The nurse practitioners, of course, said nothing. By the end of the session Mr. Escobar was destined for blood tests for renal function and glycosylated hemoglobin (a test representing average glucose levels over time), a baseline EKG for evidence of previous or current heart attack, and urine tests for protein and glucose. Recommendations for ophthalmologic examination, nephrology consultation, and endocrinology input were also made but discarded as impractical. His simple clinic visit for a prescription refill had become a two-hour, four-hundred-dollar ordeal. But the worst was yet to come.

"We thank you for your time, Mr. Escobar, and wish you good luck," said Sargent formally. "Dr. Midlin has just one other very important task and you will be on your way to the lab and the pharmacy." With this, she shot yet another glare in Midlin's direction which was framed by the smiles of the other trainees in the room. Of course! Midlin was horrified by this demonstration of yet another omission, for he had not performed Sargent's favorite examination—the one she believed no male patient should ever be allowed to leave the clinic without. Mr. Escobar's prostate gland had not been felt, nor had his stool been tested for hidden blood. As the group filed out of the room Midlin prepared the jelly, glove and stool test card for the examination but found he was unable to find the right words to prepare Mr. Escobar. Ultimately with grunts and graphic hand signals he was able to convince his hapless charge to drop his pants, turn around, and then endure much worse.

As Midlin hustled out of the room to rejoin the group he heard Tees and Sargent in conversation and was somewhat surprised at the content. Midlin had been mentally berating himself for his inattention to Sargent's favorite details—he had been distracted by the seeming simplicity of the case and had failed to apply the universally applicable lists of his esteemed mentor. Tees, on the other hand, seemed to have a different opinion.

"I'm confused," Tees was saying. "If diabetic retinopathy can be diagnosed and treated best by an ophthalmologist and yearly ophthalmology visits are required in diabetics, why are we performing a substandard ophthalmoscope exam without pupillary dilation? Furthermore, if we find evidence of renal insufficiency, a subclinical heart attack or asymptomatic atherosclerosis of the renal or femoral vessels what will we actually be able to do?"

Sargent sighed as she gave what was to her the obvious answer. "If any such findings were present it would be an indication for more aggressive control of glucose levels and blood pressure."

Tees pointed to the chart in Midlin's hand, where Midlin had dutifully copied Mr. Escobar's dutifully recorded representative glucose values. "But look at this guy's sugars. They're better than any of ours. His blood pressure is normal. How could we improve on that?"

Sargent glowered at Tees for a moment and then said levelly, "You would want to know." Her tone clearly indicated that the conversation was over, and Tees wisely took the hint. Only Midlin heard his muttered, “Yeah, well, at four hundred bucks Mr. Escobar may not want to.”

The group was already moving on to the next clinic room, with various minions joining and leaving as the demands of their own patients dictated. The amorphous aggregation passed by the window to the waiting room, and here Sargent drew up, turned and pointed. The patient she indicated was an elderly obese man whose swollen legs could be seen from across the room and whose breathing was obviously labored. He was sitting in a tense attitude, leaning forward and perched on the edge of his chair in the typical appearance of chronic congestive heart failure. His lungs were filling with the fluids his heart was unable to pump, and for these patients breathing is hardest when lying down and easiest when standing up owing to the flow of fluid out of and into the legs. Fluid pooling in the legs takes the strain off the heart and allows the lungs to clear, and so these patients are more comfortable the more upright they were. Many such patients sleep in reclining chairs rather than beds as a result. The phenomenon is well known and had even resulted in earlier congestive heart failure patients being treated with leg tourniquets to reduce the circulating blood volume, and certainly the current handling of this situation with diuretics and blood pressure control would need to be managed today in the ER. Unable to resist a teaching point even in the face of this relative emergency Sargent asked of the group, “Anyone know what that is?”

One of the more daring nurse practitioners was ready with a diagnosis.

“A classic?” she proffered.

CHAPTER 8

If Midlin had thought the ER chaotic it was only because he had not yet rotated through the intensive care unit. The ICU specialized in the monitoring of every tiny physiologic detail coupled with immediate pharmacologic response to any shift of the patients' tenuous drug-induced equilibrium. There were large catheters in the neck veins and small catheters in the wrist arteries of every patient, and the resulting pressure waveforms were displayed and analyzed continuously on the various screens about each room. The mechanical ventilators added their chorus to the cacophony of sound, and separate but equally noisy monitors gauged each patient's core temperature, the level of oxygen in each bloodstream, and the output of each heart. As a result the whole unit rivaled a video arcade for sheer overwhelming visual and auditory stimuli, with frequent loud alarm bells and continuous blinking lights in all corners of every room. The nurses, usually assigned to one or two rooms at most, still found an insistent need to run to and fro in a continual state of panic. A persistent condition in medicine is denoted as 'status'—'status epilecpticus' is an unbreakable seizure while 'status asthmaticus' is an asthma attack intractable to treatment. Tees had described nursing activity in the ICU as 'status menstrati,' although of course Midlin actually attributed this line to Flynn.

Midlin was indeed overwhelmed by his surroundings, and adding to his discomfort was the apparent superiority of the nurses in this environment. They all could distinguish the bell of hypotension from the gong of hypoxia and were often responding to the problem before Midlin could figure out which monitor in which room was signaling which abnormality. To make Midlin even more superfluous there were standard, permanent drug orders with scaled, predetermined dosages for each potential eventuality. Each nurse was familiar with these orders, while Midlin still had not even heard of some of the various medications in use. He was glad when he sat down to review the charted histories of his various new charges and was immediately given the menial task of discharging Mr. Morgan from the ICU, paperwork being the familiar sight that it was.

Mr. Morgan had done well, having been on the ventilator for just a few days and after that making the progression to eating, drinking, urinating and defecating without the help of tubes or nurses. His pneumonia had ultimately responded to stewing in a plethora of antibiotics and Midlin had been spared the humiliation of an undiagnosed case of mummy-handlers lung. His stay had unfortunately been prolonged by a disagreement between his kidneys and some gentamicin, and while the dialysis center had provided mediation his kidneys had ultimately recovered from the insult. Midlin was acutely aware of his previous failings in Mr. Morgan's documentation and copied several pages of his nursing, laboratory, and drug orders meticulously. In the end only ten new pages went to the wards with Mr. Morgan, a surprisingly low number given such recent complications as respiratory and renal failure. With such little paperwork required for his care Mr. Morgan would clearly be back to golfing soon.

Midlin turned his attention to reviewing his new intensive care charges, trying to block out the ambient chaos and concentrate on the complex medical histories of his varied patients. He barely even noticed the names of each participant, and certainly here in the unit there were no faces to put with them anyway. Each patient looked exactly the same, a swollen sweaty slab of flesh seemingly suspended by plastic ropes and unrecognizable even to immediate family. Many rooms had pictures of the hapless patients in better times, but even these were insufficient to convince Midlin of their humanity. As he perused the charts Midlin began to see similarities even beyond the outward appearances of the various patients. Each one had come to the ICU suffering from an entirely different malady, yet all had shown a similar progression of respiratory, renal and hepatic failure that was remarkably alike in each case.

Mr. Redding had had atherosclerosis for much of his 72 years, and when his abnormally dilated and plaque-encrusted abdominal aorta had finally burst he had been transported via helicopter almost straight to the operating room. A sterile and expensive Dacron tube was sewn into place as a substitute, and as exciting as this was it was only the beginning of Mr. Redding's adventure. In spite of well-established data showing his chances of returning to normal life to be well below 1% no expense or effort had been spared. He had remained on the ventilator for the forty-eight hours following surgery and so the ICU staff was spared the need to intubate him again when the first effects of adult respiratory distress syndrome (ARDS) began to manifest themselves. Initially described in and as "Danang" lung, this disorder was first seen in severely injured

Vietnam soldiers and occurs as a result of a massive release of 'inflammatory mediators' from damaged organs. These mediators consist of a variety of chemical substances with names such as prostaglandin and bradykinin and are the same culprits which cause the swelling in a sprained ankle. In cases of massive tissue damage, however, these chemicals have more than local effects and ultimately converge on the lungs due to the organization of the body's venous drainage. Here they have much the same effect as in the ankle, and this "swelling" takes the form of fluid accumulation in the air sacs of the lungs. This disorder was not seen in the days before emergent fluid resuscitation as any patient in the past hurt badly enough to suffer such a release of inflammatory mediators simply died at the scene. The Vietnam War, however, saw such improvement in emergency care that many such patients survived the trip to the MASH only to develop respiratory failure in the coming two days. The need to overcome the effects of this fluid was in turn the inspiration for the development of positive-pressure ventilation, and now both the disorder and its widely applicable treatment were omnipresent in the intensive care unit.

Although Mr. Redding's tissue damage was due to aortic and not artillery shell rupture, his hypotension and ischemic tissue damage as well as his inflammatory mediator release and lung damage had followed the same sequence as if he had been caught exposed in a rice paddy. His lungs had filled with tenacious fluid and continued mechanical ventilation had been required, air being unable to reach the lung's air sacs without the aid of pressurization. He had now completed his first week on the ventilator and so had reached an important ICU milestone. The inflated cuff of the endotracheal tube applies such pressure to the walls of the trachea that blood flow is impaired and necrosis and, ultimately, scarring result in less than two weeks. Because of this Mr. Redding would be fitted with a tracheostomy tube in the coming days, a minor surgical procedure implanting a tube directly into the windpipe. Mr. Redding could then relax and wait for his kidneys and liver to fail. Ironically enough, his Dacron aorta substitute was working admirably.

The next chart was slightly thicker, and accordingly Mr. James had been a guest in the ICU for a little longer than Mr. Redding. Mr. James had arrived in the ICU with a severe pneumonia on his chest x-ray which had defied all efforts at specific diagnosis. He had failed to improve with a variety of simultaneous antibiotics and all the attempts to culture an offending bacterial agent from his sputum, blood, and urine had failed. According to the oldest of medical traditions he had thus been deemed victim of a "virus." Although expensive tests for specific viruses remained negative this diagnosis persisted. Only a few of the thousands of viruses could actually be specifically sought in the laboratory, the remainder being uncommon, having no test commercially available, or not yet identifiable by modern microbiologists. As the more focal blob of white on his x-ray quickly changed to a diffuse white reflecting the accumulation of fluid throughout his lungs, an ICU room and ventilator were reserved for Mr. James indefinitely and the diagnosis ARDS was added to his problem list. As days stretched into a week he had shown a predictable but ominous rise in his blood urea nitrogen and creatinine. These chemicals are eliminated by the kidneys and are the laboratory hallmark of kidney failure. The subsequent buildup of metabolic byproducts and fluid retention had greatly complicated the management of his respiratory failure, as excess fluid from any source will often ultimately accumulate in the lungs. The fluid and byproducts were now removed by a dialysis machine every other day. In the interval the pressures in his pulmonary circulation and heart were monitored by a pulmonary arterial catheter, and in response to the columns of numbers produced Mr. James was given the appropriate amounts of either fluid or diuretic medication.

His renal failure was also the result of inflammatory mediator release, only much delayed relative to the failure of his lungs. The same substances which had converged on his lungs to cause his initial need for ventilator support had continued to circulate and had ultimately reached his kidneys in lesser but no less deadly concentrations. The release of those mediators had occurred throughout his body, and the effects of the same phenomenon have been felt in the muscles of anyone who has suffered from a milder form of 'the flu.' The myoglobin and other muscle enzymes released in such an infection certainly contributed to Mr. James' kidney problems by precipitating in the delicate renal filter system, but the 10-day delay in the onset of symptoms showed the real culprit to be his own body's attempt to cure itself of the virus with prostaglandin and bradykinin.

Midlin now reached across the counter for his third chart but found he couldn't lift it with one hand. As he slid it along the counter he saw the stamp '4th of 4' on the cover and realized he would be unable to lift Mr. Domer's entire medical record with both arms, knees bent, and his back straight. Mr. Domer's chart was baffling to Midlin, not just because of the vast amount of information contained therein but also because of the obvious futility of his case. He was yet to see obvious futility enter into medical decision making this year, and he had admittedly been surprised by a few recoveries his inexperienced eye had determined impossible. All the same, the concerted efforts of every subspecialty service in the hospital had revealed tumor cells in every organ of Mr. Domer's body. There was so much tumor that no one could determine where it had originally begun, a fact causing some confusion in the exact approach to his treatment. The tumors in his brain had made him demented and partly paralyzed, the tumors in his chest made him laboriously short of breath, the tumors in his abdomen gave him incessant pain, and the tumors in his bones had resulted in several fractures while he lay in bed. His large Catholic family had provided a picture of him which hung in his room, depicting a strapping 40-year-old with a big smile, bigger biceps, and a giant backpack. Midlin wondered if perhaps this was part of the problem, for this picture bore no resemblance to the 80-year-old, tumor-ridden, ventilated, catheterized mass now accumulating bills at a base rate of $5000 a day. While the family probably didn't expect Mr. Domer to once again become the man in the picture, certainly their choice of that portrait showed their expectations to be unreasonable.

Mr. Domer had arrived escorted by a legion of oncologists. The chart seemed to indicate that the tumor specialists had behaved like drunken bartenders, pouring a little chemotherapy from each of their many bottles and producing a cytotoxic Long Island iced tea. In spite of the variety of chemotherapy drugs available (in a variety of colors, even) all the medications had one common characteristic: they were poison. The theory behind chemotherapy is that a tumor cell is undergoing rapid, uncontrolled growth and thus has nutritional requirements many times that of a normal cell. Just as the hungriest of hogs dies first when poison is swilled into the slop trough so go the tumor cells when the chemotherapy is delivered. Complications arise because even normal cells vary greatly in their consumption habits, and as every class has a jovial fat kid so every body has bone marrow and gut lining cells to fall victim to their own gluttony. These cells show the highest growth, reproduction, and death rates in the normal body and so obviously bear the brunt of intravenous toilet cleaner administration, sucking the colorful stuff up at rates approaching those of the voracious tumor cells themselves. Like the civilians of Hiroshima or Dresden they are sacrificed for a greater good.

Chemotherapy doses are calculated according to

sophisticated formulae based on the patient's mass, renal function, and body surface area (itself determined by a sophisticated formula). In spite of this apparent precision the effects of these drugs are highly unpredictable, and the degree of suffering induced in each patient varies greatly. The vast majority of the bone marrow and gut lining cells die, and while in almost every case they regrow in three weeks those long days are spent oozing blood from both ends of a raw digestive tract and without the benefit of red blood cell, white blood cell, and platelet replenishment to combat anemia, fight infection, or allow for blood clotting. The bone marrow cell death was often referred to as "dose-limiting toxicity" by the frustrated oncologists, and it was this that gave rise to the barbaric modification of bone marrow transplantation. In cases where chemotherapy doses beyond this safety margin are desired, a representative sample of the bone marrow is extracted from the pelvis and stored in the freezer while the patient is steeped in seemingly fatal doses of toxins. With great ceremony and a funny smell the frozen marrow is later thawed and returned to the patient by intravenous injection, and it incredibly travels through the veins to repopulate the now-vacant marrow spaces of the bones. While this extravagant procedure has been shown to be very effective in certain childhood leukemias, its generalized application to the adult cancer population has resulted in the impressive prolongation of agony, expenditure, and hospital stays but not necessarily of life.

Whatever the circumstances of chemotherapy administration, bone marrow transplant or routine tumor treatment, the effects of bone marrow death (euphemistically referred to as "suppression") consume the thoughts and energies of the entire medical establishment. The lack of red blood cells results in fatigue and even ischemic damage to the heart and brain, for it deprives these organs of oxygen just as surely as a clogged artery would. This is treated with frequent expensive blood transfusions and expensive hormonal stimulation of the remaining marrow cells. The absence of white blood cells results in widespread infections, often due to the seemingly innocuous organisms that normally dwell in the gut or on the skin surface. These fungal and parasitic as well as viral and bacterial infections require treatment with unusual, potent, and expensive antimicrobial medications. Lastly, the absence of platelets and thus of normal blood clotting results in the constant oozing of blood from the nose, gums, and denuded gastrointestinal tract in the luckier patients and in massive brain or gastrointestinal hemorrhage in the less fortunate. This absence, too, is treated with regular and expensive transfusions, each of which shows diminishing effect as the body's battered immune system comes to recognize and remove the foreign platelets.

Mr. Domer had received his chemotherapy cocktail with nothing more than the most severe nausea and vomiting of his life, so dramatic it had precluded drinking, eating, sleeping or even coherent thought. His oncologists were pleased with what was to them an uneventful start to his therapy. Their satisfied smiles fell two days later when Mr. Domer began struggling to breathe, several days before anyone expected his true misery to begin. His chest x-ray showed nothing but white fluid where black aerated lungs should have been, but it still was some time before the diagnosis of chemotherapy-induced ARDS was established since such entities as congestive heart failure and severe pneumonia can have an identical radiographic appearance. The poisoned cells of his body had released their inflammatory mediators as enthusiastically as if he had been shot by Cong or infected by virus, and Mr. Domer was on his way to the unit.

Once in the intensive care unit Mr. Domer's bone marrow "suppression" took on a whole new level of significance. His various catheter sites oozed thin runny blood at all hours. When this was mopped up the skin redness and purulent discharge of infection was often revealed underneath, and as a result the catheters were changed with almost daily regularity. The ensuing needle assaults caused more bleeding and yet were still insufficient to prevent the development of a bloodstream infection with subsequent predictable infection of his rickety 80-year-old heart valves. This new central location for the various infectious organisms, the microbiologic equivalent to a penthouse on Central Park, allowed them unfettered access to Mr. Domer's entire body. He had developed abscesses in every conceivable location, seeding infectious material carried by his bloodstream not only into his minimal remaining normal tissue but also into the tumor cells now masquerading as his spleen, liver, bones and brain. Unfortunately for him and so many similar patients the constant infusions of antibiotics were never enough to eradicate infection as functional white blood cells are required for that definitive effect. Instead, the antibiotics were intended only to keep him alive until his bone marrow began producing white blood cells once again. Mr. Domer and the ICU staff weren't the only ones anxiously awaiting the return of his leukocytes, for an oncologist checked in every day to see if Mr. Domer's blood counts had recovered enough for him to receive more chemotherapy. The subsequent failings of his kidneys and liver in the coming weeks had surprised no one as Mr. Domer had so little functional organ tissue remaining anyway.

Midlin rubbed his weary eyes and looked up from the stack of charts before him. The unaccustomed sights and sounds of the unit once again penetrated his consciousness, and he realized how complete his concentration on the various charts had been. He also realized how completely excluded from the proceedings he was—in spite of the persistent alarm bells and lights he had not been consulted on a single issue for the two hours he had been reading. He had come in early to prepare himself for rounds and was now ready to discuss each patient's case in great detail, however, so he was grateful that he had gone unmolested. He had, he thought, mastered the extensive histories of each patient including prior surgeries, underlying illnesses, and medications and was ready to contribute to medical decisions as well as answer any questions put to him by the attending physician.

The clock read 8:00 and there was a generalized milling about that suggested the beginnings of rounds. Midlin saw Tees and Robbins in amongst a horde of nurses, technicians, and pharmacists and guessed that they were his colleagues assigned to ICU that month. The three of them stood together to one side of the large group and awaited the ICU attending, Dr. Killion. All of them were expecting the typical rapid-fire questioning on patient data and medical knowledge known as "pimping" and all of them were nervous. Medical rounds on the inpatient wards were a more informal affair, usually led by a senior resident and amounting to a friendly discussion of medical management among a handful of interns and medical students. This gathering for ICU rounds was unlike anything that Midlin had ever seen, and he dreaded the upcoming public display of his inadequacy. It appeared that every member of the hospital's ancillary services was there to witness the debacle, and just as Dr. Killion entered Midlin noticed a janitor surreptitiously stow his mop and bucket and join the fringes of the crowd.

Midlin relaxed at the start of rounds, however, as it became immediately apparent that no one would be asking anything of the interns today. Midlin had come prepared to discuss the fascinating origins of the various diseases and organ failures they were battling but he was apparently alone in this desire. Dr. Killion, looking as tired and haggard as an anchorman on election night, merely presided over the mob scene and asked no questions of anyone. He had clearly just rolled out of bed, and his obvious intention was to endure rounds without coming fully awake. He observed the proceedings passively through half-closed eyelids and allowed the nurses and various technicians to lead the discussion of each patient's care. The interns found themselves gradually huddling closer and closer together as they realized, like three blacks at a cross-burning, how completely out of place they were. The discussion was in a language of brand names and acronyms that they barely understood and it centered on aspects of medical care they had never fully realized existed.

For the most part, the discussion was about catheters. These initially sterile, flexible rubber tubes were omnipresent in the ICU. Every trachea had an endotracheal tube, every bladder had a balloon-tipped catheter, every nose and stomach had one end of a nasogastric tube, every wrist artery had a pressure-transducer-tipped tube, and in every large vein latex and blood shared space and time. Less fortunate patients might require additional catheters in areas of particular concern: tubes in the chests of pneumonia or trauma patients, tubes in the delicate ventricles of the brain in head injury and neurosurgery patients, tubes in the pulmonary arteries of heart failure patients, and drainage tubes in the surgical sites of the Phillistines' latest trampling grounds. The various tubes allowed for constant monitoring of every conceivable biologic parameter as well as unrestricted access to every body fluid, to the extent that the most carefully monitored patients could develop anemia as they bled into laboratory tubes. The factual data produced by these interminable samplings were largely ignored on rounds, however, and the group's focus was on the catheters themselves. The management of these sacred icons was fraught with difficulty, for any such persistent indwelling device provided a conduit for bacterial migration and subsequent infection. The management of an ICU patient therefore became a question of which tubes had been in which places for how long and which ones therefore should be replaced, moved, or changed to a more expensive brand. When Midlin wanted to discuss the causes of Mr. James' renal failure the group debated the timing of his dialysis treatment and the status of his high-flow dialysis catheter. Midlin stood to attention ready to comment on the prognosis for Mr. Domer's tumor-ridden body but only the seemingly impossible clotting and resultant uselessness of his femoral venous catheter was mentioned.

Rounds ended much as they had begun, with people simply drifting away as they lost interest or were distracted by alarm bells. Midlin was disappointed in his first ICU rounds for he had rather hoped for spirited discourse of the pathology and physiology playing out before their eyes. He had instead endured commentary more fitted to a plumber's convention and could recall no recent additions to his medical knowledge. One glance at the stacks of accordioned flowsheets in each patient room made Midlin reconsider, however. The rows and columns of these five-foot sheets were filled with numbers every day, and it would take a sophisticated computer program to make any logical analysis of it. Given his own current feelings of inadequacy he was ultimately glad to have been spared the additional effort of analyzing this data, and he vowed to begin learning algorithms and catheter brand names for next morning's rounds.

CHAPTER 9

Midlin was nominally in charge of ICU admissions today, reporting directly to the attending physician without the intervening supervision of a resident in a new and unusual reorganization of the medical hierarchy. He stood alone in the center of the room for a few minutes after the conclusion of rounds but found there was no call for his presence. Robbins, in charge of management issues today, had already joined the scampering crowds of nurses. Killion, called in the night before for several admissions, was now occupying Midlin's bed in the call room. Midlin was forced to pass the time at the nurses' station attempting to memorize algorithms from a nursing textbook with numerous pictures. All the while he could feel the cold touch of the ICU admission pager newly attached to his belt, constantly threatening to convert him from idleness to frenzied activity. Midlin found himself thinking of Sargent, for it was exactly in this kind of situation that her presence was welcome. She would at this moment be drilling Midlin in differential lists and algorithms had she been present, but unfortunately the senior resident position in the ICU had been eliminated and Midlin was left with a medical comic book as his only source of inspiration.

This arrangement was new this year, and was the direct result of the Medicare witch hunt currently sweeping the nation. The year before, the University of Pennsylvania had been crucified on the legal cross for all academic medical centers to see, and the academic community was hastily covering its tracks and altering its schedules to avoid catching the eye of these greedy federal accountants with a fresh scent in their nostrils. The prosecution of U Penn for millions of dollars in Medicare fraud was a little like arresting a college student for marijuana possession, for every single academic center in the country practiced in exactly the same way. Academic physicians received far lower salaries than their counterparts in private practice—as little as one-fourth the salary in some specialties. In exchange, these physicians worked a lighter schedule and endured no overnight call. This arrangement was intended to give these doctors the time to engage in their various research interests, and was made possible by the presence of residents. The residents handled all of the overnight admissions and emergencies to then have their performance critiqued the coming morning. As there was a supervision hierarchy within the residency itself this system rarely resulted in uncorrectable errors, and truly this near-continuous practice often made the senior residents superior to the attending physicians in procedures and emergency management. All the same, every resident had at some time had his management plans completely altered come the light of day and all had begun at least one embarrassing speech with the words, "Well, Mrs. Jones, we have decided to change your medications and order different tests…"

Medicare officials had only recently become aware of this system, or at least had only recently become aware that a large amount of money could be reclaimed as a result of it. All admissions, treatment decisions and procedures performed in the hospital were theoretically to be supervised by an attending physician, while in reality of course most of this activity was performed by residents alone. The addition of the attending physician's signature to the chart the next morning was sufficient inspiration for the hospital to charge Medicare accordingly, with all parties turning a blind eye to the actual physical absence of that physician at the decisive moment. This practice had been universal throughout academic centers since the days of Osler[6], even though under strict legal scrutiny it constituted fraud. The clever Medicare staff had decided to provide this legal scrutiny and an extensive review of hospital records began with the unfortunate University of Pennsylvania. Accusations and massive fines were subsequently levied and a fearful and dramatic change in academic health care delivery occurred overnight. Now all hospitals required the presence of attending physicians for all significant activities and the joys of an academic position had paled accordingly. Gone were the days of sleep and ease, and gone with them the days of idle time spent in research. Instead, academic physicians regularly found themselves in the hospital overnight for the supervision of admissions and procedures and the vast increase in their work hours saw no accompanying increase in their paltry salaries. The result had been an exodus of these professors to greener pastures and a further increase in workload on those

---

[6] Considered the father of modern medical diagnosis, this famous professor hailed from the Johns Hopkins School of Medicine near the turn of the century. Ironically, in this age of technologic advancement his techniques of physical examination are anything but modern.

few remaining. In addition, the quality of education had declined as the more qualified physicians found desirable private practice jobs and the residents were deprived of the important instructional element of autonomy.

Nowhere in the hospital had this shift in responsibilities been more poignantly felt than in the intensive care unit. The previous staff of five attendings had dropped to two in just a few short months, and those that had remained had found themselves exhausted, overworked, and with nonexistent home lives. The hospital had eliminated the presence of a resident in the ICU with the reasoning that the attending physician was required for supervision anyway and the redundant resident, previously useful in that supervisory role, could be better employed elsewhere in the hospital clinics. There had as yet been no admissions or procedures that day, and as a result Killion was sleeping soundly rather than teaching Midlin.

The three interns in the unit that month had already agreed on their rotating assignments, with Tees drawing the lucky straw and being assigned the off-duty "post-call" status that day even though he had not been sleepless the night before. He was, of course, already gone and most likely enjoying the company of one of his nurse harem. The remaining intern, Robbins, was a mousy and meticulous woman with whom Midlin had had little dealings with so far this year. She was infamous for her dedication, often seen wandering the hospital late into the evening even on her theoretic off-duty, "post-call" days; days on which Tees was long departed by noon. Her paperwork was performed in a small, calligraphic hand and omitted not even the smallest detail. In contrast, she rarely spoke of the details of her personal life and Midlin had come to assume that there were none.

Midlin watched Robbins attempt to aid in the care of the unit patients. She was ostensibly there for a regular eight-hour day in an "overflow" capacity, helping with routine care issues while Midlin was occupied with admissions or procedures. Of course, she had taken her duties to heart and had arrived as early as Midlin had that morning. Midlin was grateful for her presence and at first had attributed the lack of recent interruptions to her assistance. As he watched her run from room to room in response to the indecipherable alarms, though, he realized she was as superfluous as he knew himself to be. She reminded him of an unwanted younger sibling, tagging along with the older children and being rudely dismissed with each belated arrival. The only reason he had not been interrupted was that no one cared what he or Robbins thought. Each nurse carried with her a collection of laminated vomit-, blood-, and urine-proof cards on which were printed a variety of treatment algorithms. Consultation with these rather than with interns was the preferred method of decision-making. These holy tablets (prepared by nurses, pharmacists, and doctors in consultation) had seemingly eliminated the need for independent thought and coupled with standing orders for a variety of drugs they gave the ICU nurses a spectacular degree of professional if not intellectual autonomy. Midlin saw Robbins try to steal a look at the cards over a nurse's shoulder more than once, and he wondered himself where he could get a set. Maybe Tees had a connection.

Midlin's peripheral observation of the scene was interrupted by the one sound he could recognize: the ICU admission pager. He fumbled for a while at the assortment of noisemakers on his waistline and first pressed buttons on his personal pager and ophthalmoscope before achieving silence. His belt had come to look like Batman's, especially since he always received additional pagers upon Tees' early departure. Midlin noticed that none of the nurses looked up, the sound of the pager going unnoticed as there was no corresponding card to flip to. Some of them would care soon enough, though, as Midlin noted the ominous ER extension 6336 on the pager display. This could only portend an admission, and was a number every intern and resident had come to dread by his second month on duty. The ER was always at odds with the rest of the hospital as they were primarily responsible for the admission and disposition of patients, and so a page to this extension could only mean an increase in the workload of the testy respondent. Midlin tried to sound enthusiastic as he answered the page and discussed his first ICU admission with a defensive ER resident. It was Oggler, a usually jovial and always-hungry resident who Midlin thought should have a run at Sargent.

Despite her relatively young age, Mrs. Langer had lain in her living room under a shawl for the entire afternoon while knitting a sweater for her granddaughter (also despite her relatively young age), and when her bladder was near to bursting she finally rose, stretched, and started across the room. She had hit the floor quickly and fortunately turned blue rather slower, so that when the ambulance arrived she had only begun to turn a dusky steel color around the mouth. The paramedics administered the value package of medical instrumentation, and Mrs. Langer was quickly receiving saline through an IV and oxygen through an endotracheal tube. Her oxygen saturation and blood pressure hovered at 90% and 90 mmHg respectively; both considered just enough to sustain life without organ damage. On her arrival at the ER Oggler's job was made easy, for any patient with marginal vital signs such as these would require the extensive monitoring only the ICU could provide. The degree to which Oggler considered himself removed from the scene was apparent when Midlin heard him laugh over the phone.

"Hey, man, her charts just got here," he chuckled. "Took three clerks and two carts to tote them up here. I'll just send them straight up there with her." It was true that with Mrs. Langer's ultimate destination so obviously decided a review of her extensive medical data by the ER physician would be pointless, but Midlin found Oggler's hilarity less than infectious. He hung up and awaited the train of gurneys, machinery, monitors, and chart carts that would herald Mrs. Langer's arrival.

Midlin knew he would have to call Killion at some point for his supervision of not only Mrs. Langer's treatment decisions but also the placement of her central venous and arterial catheters. There would be a patient to examine, piles of charts to peruse, and management orders to write as well and Midlin was concerned about the timing of his call. Too early and the attending would lose precious sleep and be annoyed, too late and patient welfare and Medicare fraud would become considerations. The nurses were of no help at all, mostly giving Midlin blank stares at his mention of an attending physician before returning to card flipping and injecting. The chaos was so extreme when the admission entourage arrived seconds later that Midlin broke down and aroused Killion from sleep with a page.

Midlin's first impression was that Killion was annoyed but soon came to realize he was only tired, hurried, and obsessed with returning to his cot. He arrived quickly after a hasty job of dressing and no attempt at all at concealing his midday bedhead. He ignored Midlin and the stacks of charts being piled on the counters and went straight to the patient's family members uncertainly collected at the entrance to Mrs. Langer's new accommodations. He interviewed them as a group for a few minutes amidst the bustle of Mrs. Langer's bed transfer, and then with his stethoscope listened once over each of her lungs. A fast look beneath the bed sheets followed, and then just as quickly Killion joined Midlin at the counter.

"This lady's had a PE," he stated definitively, circumventing the traditional interactive medical education process and in his haste even forced to abbreviate "pulmonary embolus." "We'll get her lines in then heparinize her, and as long as her lungs stay clear you can dump fluid in her." With this he placed his feet on the counter and waited for the nurses to put the finishing sheet tucks on Mrs. Langer's cot and herd the family members into the waiting room. The didactic portion of Midlin's ICU instruction was apparently at an end.

Mrs. Langer had formed a large clot in the femoral vein of her leg, due mostly to the stasis of the blood in that vein as she lay under her shawl. For this same reason clot formation was the bane of immobilized hospital patients and had led to the invention of a variety of mostly ineffective leg-squeezing devices for those immobile patients considered to be at risk. When Mrs. Langer rose to stretch that soft, gooey, newly formed clot had broken free from the vessel wall and traveled to the right atrium, right ventricle, pulmonary artery, and ultimately the lungs like a log dropped in a river. When the clot had finally reached a pulmonary arterial branch too small to permit passage it had lodged, and the subsequent blockage had caused dramatic changes in the interrelated pressures of the great vessels and heart chambers. A pulmonary embolus puts increased strain on the right side of the heart and results in a drop in blood pressure but relatively clear lungs, while a heart attack affects the more muscular and blood-hungry left side and the ensuing fluid backup results in pulmonary edema. Fluid resuscitation is effective in right-sided heart failure but can be dangerous in the more severe cases of left-sided heart failure. The classic story of immobilization followed by acute onset of symptoms had convinced Killion as to the nature of Mrs. Langer's right-sided heart problem even before he had listened to her clear lungs or spotted her swollen leg.

Mrs. Langer would be receiving heparin for the next few days in order to prevent the formation of more clots in either her leg or her lungs. Heparin, a normal product of the liver, is harvested from a variety of barnyard animal organ preparations and is administered intravenously. It binds to the blood's clotting factors and prevents formation of new thrombus but does nothing to dissolve clot already in existence. The body has its own system of thrombolysis, a series of enzymes always in balance with the thrombogenic enzymes that give rise to clot formation. These thrombolytic enzymes would ultimately break down small clots and bore holes in large ones, re-establishing the flow both to the lungs and from the legs in the coming weeks. While some more potent thrombolytic preparations are available from the tireless efforts of genetic scientists and their pharmaceutical backers, the fatal specter of associated cerebral or gastrointestinal hemorrhage always overshadows their use and in reality most patients with a clot so large as to require a thrombolytic will die before reaching the hospital. The plan, then, was for heparin to prevent new clots, the ventilator and IV fluids to maintain oxygenation and blood pressure, and Mrs. Langer's own enzymes to recanalize her vessels in due time. In the near future she would be changed to the oral anticoagulant coumadin. Discovered when a herd of cows died bloody deaths from spoiled sweet clover silage in the 1920's, coumadin was used as a rat poison until an uneventful suicide attempt suggested possible medical uses. The conversion from intravenous liver pate to oral rat poison usually took place on the third to fifth day, when an endotracheal tube no longer prevented the patient from taking a pill.

Midlin would have liked to discuss the possibility of an underlying predisposition to clot formation with his new attending. This was an opportunity to impress that every intern relished, for a list of congenital thrombolytic enzyme deficiencies, autoimmune diseases, underlying cancers and their respective diagnostic lab tests was at the tip of every aspiring new doctor's tongue when confronted with a case of thrombosis. Killion was quite obviously only interested in returning to bed, however, and dismissed Midlin's diagnostic overtures with a wave of his hand. There was a fast lesson in central venous and arterial catheter placement that amounted to a hurried flash of needles and wires and then Killion was back in Midlin's bed in the call room. Mrs. Langer was similarly though less comfortably tucked in, with tracings of her blood pressure and oxygenation dancing across her monitor screens. Midlin was left alone with a tall stack of paperwork and taller stacks of charts. He signed his name to the bottom of each page of standard medication orders and noted no allowance for alterations was made on any of the forms. Performing the one individualized act in Mrs. Langer's care, Midlin took out a form for the administration of heparin and signed the bottom. Rather than a distinctive alarm bell the nurses would respond to a test of the blood's coagulation time known as the PTT. The normal PTT of 20-30 would be increased to 80-100 by a single dose or "bolus" of heparin and then maintained there by a continuous intravenous infusion. The initial dose would be calculated by the nurse and the infusion rate determined in response to the frequent PTT tests. Midlin's contribution was apparently over, and he turned his attention to Mrs. Langer's daunting charts.

Midlin saw immediately why Mrs. Langer had come with so much baggage. She was suffering from systemic lupus erythematosis (SLE), the queen mother of autoimmune diseases. While there were many diseases in which the body attacked its own tissues with antibodies, in fact as many such diseases as there are types of tissue, lupus is unusual in that it affects a variety of tissue types in a variety of combinations. Patients can suffer rashes, bone marrow suppression with low blood cell counts, renal failure, and neurologic damage to name just a few manifestations. Such antibody attacks are probably initiated by an infection—the body attempts to make infection-specific antibodies to a viral or bacterial protein that resembles normal body tissue on a molecular level. The antibodies produced bind to friend and foe indiscriminately and self-induced organ damage results. Analogous disorders include heart valve damage in the face of streptococcal infection (rheumatic heart disease), thyroid destruction associated with a number of viral infections (Hashimoto's thyroiditis), and neurologic damage from multiple sclerosis and joint damage from rheumatoid arthritis (each an immune response to an unknown agent). Midlin had come to view the diagnosis of lupus with some skepticism, for the disease was known for its ability to mimic other disorders and was notoriously difficult to diagnose precisely. He was also very familiar with lupus, for there was an established list of thirteen diagnostic criteria in all the textbooks that Sargent loved to close her eyes and recite. The more he read of Mrs. Langer's charts the more convinced he became that this truly was her problem. She had developed effusions regularly, fluid collections in the pleural spaces of her chest and in the pericardial space around her heart. She had at various times shown decreases in all types of blood cells including red cells and platelets. She had permanent red blotches from capillary skin lesions and an intermittent sloughing facial rash. Her kidneys had failed years ago and she visited the dialysis center regularly, when she wasn't visiting the medical clinic or the hospital ward. The only redeeming feature of this illness seemed to be the chronic deterioration of Mrs. Langer's mental function from autoimmune cerebritis, which kept her from fully appreciating her quandary.

Midlin looked up at last from the charts and surveyed the situation. Robbins was actually gone, a clear indication of her level of frustration as this marked her earliest departure of the year. It was seven o'clock, and Midlin decided to vacate the premises when he saw the already unbelievable commotion actually double at this traditional hour of nursing shift change. Midlin's stomach growled as he descended the stairs to the cafeteria, and he thought longingly of the fried, cheesy, and gravy-laden offerings that lay before him. He had literally raved to the other members of his interview group when he had first sighted this cafeteria, to the extent that he and the others had realized that he had no other criterion on which to base his choice of residency. Midlin was the furthest thing from indulgent in this respect but he had spent many medical school nights in a room full of vending machines. He had found himself searching for dubious food group representation amongst Twix bars and Cheetos, and so had sworn to never be slave to Nabisco and Domino's as an intern. When he had seen this twenty-four hour cafeteria he had been powerless, and to eat here every day he would have done a residency in hell or even a county hospital.

Midlin saw a table of noisily congregated interns in the corner and headed for them, carrying a tray of breaded chicken on stuffing covered in sauce which rested easily on his newly forming belly. Confirming the presence of his new fat roll, his belt buckle disappeared completely from sight when he sat down next to Oggler. This objective evidence of pannus formation was shocking for Midlin, for where this tray-carrying, buckle-hiding mass now lay there had previously been nothing but skin and muscle. It had taken only five months of internship and its associated physical inactivity and unlimited food to cause this metamorphosis, and it was only small consolation to be seated next to Oggler who looked like he would soon explode. Midlin was reminded of Mrs. Langer as he looked at Oggler, for both of them had the same rounded bodies and heads with relatively slim arms and legs. This pattern of fat distribution (known as centripetal obesity) is a feature that many patients on prolonged, high dosages of steroids develop and Mrs. Langer had taken such dosages for years in an attempt to keep her lupus at bay. Oggler, of course, just ate tons of burgers and fries.

Steroids in this case refers to preparations of the adrenal hormone cortisol, a substance with widespread and profound metabolic effects which in many ways opposes the effects of insulin. A steroid in general refers to any molecule which has at its core a characteristic complex ring of carbon and oxygen atoms, impossibly named the cyclopentanoperhydrophenanthrene ring by biochemists concerned with job security. The molecules thus constructed include such widespread entities as cholesterol, vitamin D, estrogen and testosterone (the infamous 'anabolic steroid' so commonly encountered in the sporting world) as well as a variety of hormones produced by the cortex of the adrenal gland. This outer lining of the adrenal gland produces the steroid hormones aldosterone and cortisol for control of salt balance and sugar metabolism, while the central portion of the gland consists of specialized nerve cells which produce the potent substance epinephrine (known as adrenalin to the rest of the world, this hormonal classic is subject to trademark limitations in the United States). In common medical practice, the term 'steroid' always refers to high doses of the adrenal cortical steroid hormone cortisol, whose extensive metabolic effects extend even to the white cells of the immune system and cause a generalized suppression of inflammation. The doses required for this effect are often ten to twenty times the normal amount of circulating hormone, and the discovery of this effect in the 1950's altered the course of a vast number of autoimmune diseases. Patients suffering from such varied illnesses as rheumatoid arthritis, lupus, Wegener's granulomatosis, asthma, and multiple sclerosis all found immediate and almost magical relief of symptoms that previously could have progressed to fatal severity. As one would expect, these results were too good to be true and it was not long before the protean side effects of this treatment manifested.

The list of supraphysiologic cortisol's side effects is exhaustive, consistent with its normal influence on the basic processes of almost every cell in the body. As cortisol is always in balance with insulin and opposite in effect, an excess of this hormone has the same relative effect as an absence of insulin and the characteristic high blood sugars of diabetes can result. Cortisol potentiates the effects of epinephrine and accelerates many cellular processes, causing hypertension and a vast surplus of energy. Many patients are initially euphoric not just because of the abrupt cessation of their symptoms, and these mental effects of steroids can induce some to briefly cross the line into just plain crazy. Increased incidence of gastric and duodenal ulcers, necrosis of the bones of the hip, and severe osteoporosis also result, mostly due to effects on vitamin D and calcium metabolism. Some patients still remain from the early days of indiscriminate steroid use (many of whom foolishly crossed the southern border to escape the seemingly overcautious FDA), and they possess bones so leached of calcium as to be invisible to x-ray. Vertebral and hip fractures with subsequent immobilization, pneumonia, pulmonary embolism and death await these patients as surely as lung cancers and heart attacks await our smoking population. Lastly, consistent with a widespread suppression of white blood cell activity, these patients demonstrate a marked propensity to develop overwhelming infections and a troublesome delay in wound healing (abnormalities also reminiscent of diabetes).

The onset of these side effects is not the only factor complicating the dosing of cortisol. The level of cortisol in the bloodstream is constantly monitored by the pituitary gland, and this gland both causes a diurnal variation in the level of hormone and responds to decreases in cortisol with the secretion of an adrenal-stimulating substance known as ACTH (adrenocorticotropic hormone). In response to this hormone the adrenal glands grow, proliferate, and produce cortisol. If the pituitary gland senses extremely high levels of cortisol there is no ACTH release and, deprived of this hormonal prodding, the adrenal cortex withers like an unused muscle. This phenomenon begins to occur within a week of cortisol administration, and abrupt cessation of the medication at any point thereafter can result in a life-threatening absence of the hormone as the atrophied adrenals are slow to awaken from their induced hibernation. A similar phenomenon is seen with the administration of the other hormones monitored by the pituitary gland—testosterone or estrogen administration causes testicular or ovarian atrophy and thyroid hormone administration causes thyroid gland atrophy. Steroid management, therefore, is a difficult balancing act involving selection of a dose high and long enough to suppress destructive inflammation followed by a rapid but controlled dose reduction to minimize the risk of side effects but still allow for the recovery of adrenal gland function. The astute might suggest that replacement of the ACTH hormone would prevent this atrophy and still allow for high levels of cortisol, but this method of replacement is far harder to predict, manage, and monitor. End-product replacement, therefore, is the rule in endocrine hormone deficiencies.

The adrenal glands normally control the general level of activity of the body, to the degree that a small burst of cortisol around dawn probably initiates the body's awakening long before the alarm, dog, or children intervene. An abnormal adrenal response has even been demonstrated in some patients with severe depression, not surprisingly. Also predictably, the adrenal responds to any physically stressful situation such as illness or massive trauma with a large release of cortisol, an adrenal reflex not present in a patient with adrenal gland atrophy. This thought electrified Midlin when it initially crossed his mind in almost wordless form. He was still observing Oggler, who did not think this odd as he was as usual involved in an entertaining tale that would even have made Mr. Larkin blush. Oggler had clearly already been comfortable with the role of the fat jester on his arrival for internship, and the recent increase in his weight had been accompanied by a similar rise in his jocularity. Midlin, however, failed to laugh on cue as he was absorbed in thought. His pulse quickened as he realized he was about to make an important, independent contribution to Mrs. Langer's care. Oggler had behaved like a medical longshoreman in the ER, unloading her from the ambulance and bundling her off to the ICU without so much as a glance at her charts. Killion had made a snap diagnosis which most likely was correct but failed to encompass all Mrs. Langer's needs, which in this case included a large "stress dose" of steroids. Nowhere on the many ICU algorithm and standard order sheets was there mention of additional steroid doses for patients like Mrs. Langer, patients on chronic high-dose steroids with subsequent adrenal atrophy. Mrs. Langer's body was enduring a severe stress for which it required a large influx of cortisol and her shriveled adrenal glands were unable to comply. The borderline hypotension she had been displaying might at least in part be due to a relative cortisol insufficiency in addition to the effects of her pulmonary embolus, and Midlin felt his pulse quicken and his palms sweat with the realization that he had been the one to recognize it.

In his excitement Midlin felt an abrupt decrease in his appetite, and he completely lost interest in food when he noted Oggler's plate contained only a few remnants of the same smothered chicken Midlin had toted over on his own belly. Excusing himself before Oggler could begin his next story, Midlin bussed his tray and hustled back to the ICU, taking the stairs two at a time. He paused at the doors to the ICU and mopped his brow, marveling at his degree of breathlessness and resolving to begin an exercise program, perhaps on his monthly day off. The level of chaos and noise had dropped to its usual din with the departure of the previous nursing shift, and after at least half an hour of chart reviewing and discussion the new shift had settled into the accustomed routine of gathering and quantitating the viscous secretions obtained from each patient's gastric, bladder, and rectal tubes punctuated by pharmaceutical response to alarm bells. Midlin's passage to Mrs. Langer's room therefore went unnoticed.

Midlin searched Mrs. Langer's room for her chart, then continued his efforts on the countertops outside the room. The autonomous functioning of the ICU had resulted in a marked devaluing of the once-sacred medical chart, and Midlin finally found this one buried under a stack of back copies of a nursing publication entitled *Revolution; the Journal of Nursing Empowerment*. He turned to the otherwise empty section in the plastic binder for physician orders and wrote the standard dose of intravenous hydrocortisone for acute adrenal insufficiency. Knowing this would be ignored, he then sought out the nurse assigned to Mrs. Langer with the open binder in hand. Although tests exist to detect the presence of native cortisol these are expensive and unreliable due to the normal fluctuations of this hormone. The diagnosis of adrenal insufficiency is therefore somewhat intuitive and the best course is to administer a "stress dose" presumptively in the appropriate situation.

Midlin found Lisa, assigned to Mrs. Langer's care, adjusting the suction on Mrs. Langer's nasogastric tube, which kept her stomach empty of acid and other secretions. Left in the stomach, these secretions could be vomited up and breathed in past the endotracheal tube cuff, resulting in lung destruction known as aspiration pneumonia. The presence of these tubes is therefore universal in the ICU and their management mundane, but in spite of this Lisa raised a hand impatiently when Midlin tried to interrupt her. She forced him to wait while she crossed the room and recorded her latest findings on a vast flow chart which in Mrs. Langer's fourth hour in the ICU was already filling with numbers. Only then was Midlin able to draw her attention to the chart and his new order.

The order was written on the standard hospital order form. There was no color-coding and no branching diagram to identify this paper as a product of the ICU, and Lisa at first looked at it uncomprehendingly. Midlin was forced to elaborate.

"She's a steroid-dependent lupus patient so she needs stress-dosing of steroids," he explained. "It may be why she's so hypotensive."

At this Lisa showed no further evidence of understanding, and she was clearly uncomfortable to find herself in intellectual territory unmapped by algorithms. Rather than risk exposing her ignorance with further discussion she took the binder from him and turned away. As Midlin turned his attention to Mrs. Langer's flow chart he saw Lisa conferring over Midlin's order with her coworkers, all of whom displayed irritation to some degree. With no algorithmic backing, however, their ultimate decision was apparently compliance and Lisa returned to the room with a new syringe in hand.

Feeling that he had only narrowly avoided a confrontation over the recent steroid order, Midlin actually felt his heart sink with his next discovery. He had noted a subtle manifestation of a rare abnormality and should have been as excited as with his last contribution, but now as he prepared to confront the nurses in all their algorithmic might he felt only dread.

Midlin was looking at the columns reflecting Mrs. Langer's heparin dose, PTT tests, and resulting adjustments of the heparin drip rate. No matter what the drip rate Mrs. Langer's PTT tests had been the same over four hours, a markedly elevated 120 which had precipitated multiple reductions in heparin dose. The most recent reduction had been to a rate of 300mg/hr, less than one-third the typical dose and yet with no detectable change in her apparent anticoagulation. Midlin had felt the inklings of a suspicion and had looked to her first PTT test, performed prior to her initial heparin administration. It, too, was 120. This initial value told the whole story to Midlin, for it was a classic hematologic manifestation of lupus that Sargent had taught him well. Mrs. Langer was producing antibodies against the very proteins of her clotting system, and the offending antibodies were collectively referred to as "lupus anticoagulant." This apparent misnomer causes a propensity to clot formation but paradoxically reacts with laboratory agents to cause an elevated PTT, thus simulating the effects of a dose of heparin. Mrs. Langer should therefore be on a standard dose of heparin no matter what her test results, and her current dangerously low dosage would allow both clot propagation and repeated embolization.

Midlin motioned for Lisa to join him at the counter, a gesture that she clearly resented and that put her on the defensive even before Midlin began to describe the situation. He went through a careful explanation of the lupus anticoagulant phenomenon and showed Lisa the confirming laboratory values. He felt her body stiffen next to him as his intentions became clear, and this degenerated into outright head shaking when Midlin suggested increasing the heparin dose in the face of a high PTT and contrary to the instructions of the accepted algorithm. Lisa was not slow in recruiting her colleagues to her side, and they were already primed for confrontation by his last unusual order. The resulting scene was chaotic and loud even for the ICU, and a number of alarms went unnoticed as the nurses berated Midlin sarcastically for thinking himself smarter than their algorithm. With a note of finality, Midlin was informed officiously that any alterations in the standard dosage algorithms would require the input of the appropriate committees and he was free to raise the issue in the next open meeting.

Midlin went to bed that night in a narrow cot that smelled of the long-departed Killion, left with no recourse as he didn't dare call Killion in unless there was an ICU admission. He tossed and turned on his cot as he thought of his wasted day, what with his hours of chart review and conscientious attention to detail having come to nothing. He was particularly embittered because the ICU had been a career he would have considered earlier, while now he hoped only to endure this single month. When Mrs. Langer died early that morning even the application of multiple algorithms simultaneously and in succession could not save her, and understandably Midlin's presence in the corner of the room was unable to affect the outcome. He never did raise the issue in open committee meetings, for these occurred infrequently and by the next such meeting Mrs. Langer had been dead for several weeks.

CHAPTER 10

Mr. Gibson had had a stroke. This was obvious even to the nurse practitioners in the ER when they looked at the obtunded, drooling, barely arousable figure on the cot. (They knew, at least, that they were looking at a "classic.") Extreme lethargy often accompanies an acute stroke, developing in the minutes and hours following the rapid onset of painless neurological symptoms. In Mr. Gibson's case this had the typical manifestations of a large stroke involving the left motor cortex, with drooping of the left side of his face and paralysis of the opposite right arm. Also known as a cerebrovascular accident, this stroke had been anything but accidental. Atherosclerotic plaque had been building up in Mr. Gibson's carotid arteries since his late teens, and for the most part the other vessels supplying his brain (a total of two carotid and two vertebral arteries) had compensated for the steady diminution of his vascular lumens. Finally one such plaque had fissured, ruptured, or otherwise developed an irregular surface and a blood clot developed as surely as if he had cut himself shaving. That clot then separated from the vessel wall and joined the flow of blood to the brain (just like Mrs. Langer's clot, only within the oxygen-laden arterial blood and therefore much more ominous), ultimately to clog a smaller branch downstream and forever change Mr. Gibson's job prospects, athletic pursuits, and insurance premiums. This is the scenario in the vast majority of strokes, with the small remainder comprised of heart valve disease, cardiac arrhythmias, and hypercoagulable patients that would form a clot on a sheet of glass (again like Mrs. Langer). In fact, this plaque-induced clot formation is also the mechanism by which most acute heart attacks occur as well.

Midlin had been called to the ER for two reasons, both of which were apparent to him upon his arrival. The first was that Mr. Gibson looked familiar, the second that he was clearly destined for a ventilator and thus the ICU. Mr. Gibson was so lethargic his eyes never opened and he snored heavily, a sound accompanied by the gurgling of secretions in his larynx. This clearly indicated that his sedation was so complete that his swallowing reflexes were blunted, and Mr. Gibson would need an endotracheal tube to protect his lungs from a deluge of bacteria-laden saliva. Midlin was the overflow man in the ICU that day and not responsible for admissions, but Oggler had called him because Midlin knew Mr. Gibson and was ostensibly responsible for his care.

Mr. Gibson was enrolled in Midlin's Longitudinal Care Clinic, a new program within the residency intended as initiation to the joys of serial medical care. A number of patients were assigned to each intern's clinic, to be followed along for the duration of the three-year residency under supervision of an attending. The intern would handle routine doctor visits, manage medication refills, perform routine physical examinations, and administer preventive health care and counseling. The clinic was part of an effort by the Internal Medicine Department to sacrifice its earlier standing as a highly trained, hospital-oriented, cerebral specialty and become indistinguishable from other primary caregivers such as general and family practitioners. Even at this early point in the year Midlin had come to dread his weekly clinic morning, but he had so far gamely forged ahead. He had conscientiously administered drugs for cholesterol, hypertension, and diabetes; he had meticulously scheduled asymptomatic patients for regular mammography and colonoscopy; and he had felt so many prostate glands he was now disturbingly familiar with that organ's curves, fissures, and other subtle nuances. The actual amount of medicine he practiced in this clinic, however, was extremely small. Most of the clinic visits seemed to be taken up with the crying, ranting, or aimless chatting of his various healthy charges and he was rapidly coming to doubt his ability to detect even melon-sized tumors by physical examination.

Midlin felt an undeniable pang of guilt as he looked down at Mr. Gibson. Obviously every patient under sufficient longitudinal scrutiny will suffer some adverse event, but Midlin all the same felt some degree of responsibility. Here was a 60-year-old man with no significant previous medical problems and a relatively healthy lifestyle who now faced a one-sided existence as his best future prospect. As Midlin scanned Mr. Gibson's chart and refreshed his memory he became even more surprised by this sudden reversal, for Mr. Gibson showed no significant risk factors for developing atherosclerosis. He had no history of hypertension, had always shown a normal cholesterol, and was unique amongst his generation in never having smoked a day in his life. Also unusual for his age, Mr. Gibson was on no regular medications. It was this last realization that caused Midlin to draw in a sharp breath and feel his previous generalized pang of guilt become an intense feeling of nausea. This feeling grew to almost suffocating intensity as he realized that his responsibility for this event went far beyond his nominal clinic association with Mr. Gibson, for Mr. Gibson did not take a daily baby aspirin.

Aspirin was the pharmaceutical mainstay of stroke prevention. Large trials underwritten by large aspirin manufacturers had shown a 19% reduction in initial stroke events over a 5-year period, with an astounding 90% reduction in repeat events over the same time period. While aspirin in no way affects the formation of atherosclerotic plaque its value lies in its potent inhibition of platelet function. With no platelets to initially adhere to ruptured plaque the blood swirls harmlessly over previously fatal irregularities and stroke is averted. Only a small dose of aspirin is required for this effect; in fact, one-sixth of the recommended headache dose every other day is sufficient. Truly, with no specific concerning risk factors for atherosclerosis Mr. Gibson did not meet established criteria mandating aspirin therapy, but Midlin was well aware that just being a middle-aged white male suggested Mr. Gibson had at least some irregularity of his vessel walls. In spite of the rationalization value of the official criteria, therefore, Midlin felt he had been remiss. At essentially no cost and no risk of side effects Mr. Gibson could have taken a single baby aspirin a day and could right now have a 20% greater chance of protecting his own airway from saliva.

As effective as aspirin can be, Mr. Gibson's needs were now beyond its relatively weak antiplatelet offerings. Mr. Gibson had fragments of clot in both his carotid and his more distal middle cerebral arteries, either of which could propagate and worsen his already serious condition with further reduction in arterial blood flow. He would now need a CT scan of his head to exclude the presence of blood within the affected part of his brain, and if no such blood were present he would receive a bolus and infusion of heparin. Larger strokes involving the cortex of the brain have a tendency to undergo "hemorrhagic conversion" or bleeding, and this determination is extremely important in managing these patients. Prior to the existence of the CT scan such hemorrhage was detected by clinical signs such as the presence of pain or progressive symptoms, but this approach amounted to educated guessing at best. Even a small drop of bleeding could become a disastrous, massive hemorrhage under the influence of potent anticoagulants and put the finishing touches on an already miserable fate. Fortunately, such a drop could now be identified and exclude some patients from anticoagulant therapy, although surprisingly the dying portion of the brain itself cannot be identified by CT for up to a day. The actual size of the stroke could be inferred by examination but would not really be known until that time.

Midlin waited with Mrs. Gibson, spending the time looking at the floor and hoping that she was not as acutely aware of the preventive value of aspirin as he was. Mr. Gibson's return from the radiology department coincided with the arrival of the "stroke team," a conglomeration of neurologists, nurses, and pharmacologists specifically chosen to respond to cases of acute stroke. Their job was essentially to correlate the patient's history and physical examination findings with his laboratory and radiologic studies and determine his candidacy for the Rolls Royce of anticoagulants: tissue plasminogen activator (tPA). This drug is a genetically engineered offshoot of the earlier urokinase and streptokinase bacterial products, and although all three preparations were equivalent in strength a suspicious FDA intervention had left tPA in sole control of the vast market. The drug, given with heparin, is able to lyse clots already formed in contrast to heparin infusion which prevents existent clots from growing. This feature makes it extremely valuable in restoring flow to deprived heart or brain tissue, but administration of this drug merits careful deliberation as it performs its action indiscriminately throughout the body. Little clots continuously form unnoticed in small rents throughout every normal vascular system, and tPA removes all of these thumbs from the dyke with the subsequent potential for massive hemorrhage. Furthermore, the degree of improvement is directly related to the amount of time elapsed since the beginning of symptoms. Patients beyond the six-hour limit rarely benefit significantly, a fact which led to the memorable advertisement "*time is muscle.*" The decision to administer the drug is therefore fraught with difficulty and is based on a number of unquantifiable variables including time elapsed, size of stroke, and a history of recent surgery or trauma (How extensive? How recent?). The cost, ostensibly not a deciding factor, is easily quantified at several thousand dollars per dose.

Mr. Gibson had spent six hours trying to convince his wife that he was fine through the side of his mouth that was still under volitional control, and further delays at the triage desk due to a lack of visible superficial hemorrhage then ensued. By the time Mr. Gibson returned from the radiology department bearing a scribbled and curt "negative" on his CT report form over ten hours had elapsed, and upon realizing this the "stroke team" disbanded rather disconsolately. While Midlin had seen effective use of tPA for a number of acute heart attacks he wondered if he would ever see an acute stroke patient meet the extensive criteria and actually receive the drug.

Mr. Gibson never suffered hemorrhagic conversion and progressed through the predictable stages of an uncomplicated stroke. His severe lethargy gradually resolved, and subsequently his sedative and paralytic infusions were decreased until he was awake and strong enough to breathe on his own. His endotracheal tube was then deflated and removed and he began the slow and prolonged rehabilitation process, showing the typical course of gradual improvement with a marked plateau at approximately three weeks. He would always have a slack face with a tendency to drool, and his handwriting would show a deterioration similar to Nelson's after Tenerife[7]. His presence in the ICU during that first week, however, served as Midlin's inspiration for his upcoming performance in the Longitudinal Care Clinic, for Midlin still had a guilty pause every time he met Mr. Gibson's glassy eyes.

The Longitudinal Clinic began as many others had, with Dr. Cringen calling together his contingent of interns and nurse practitioners and giving them a 15-minute extemporaneous lecture on his favorite subject. Depression: everybody has it, could kill themselves because of it, and should be on medications for it. Midlin discovered even his newfound enthusiasm begin to fade towards the end of the bleak presentation and he wondered briefly if he should be medicated, but he soon refocused his energy with his first patient appointment.

Mrs. Dempsey was a fifty-year-old woman with three grown children. She was concerned about her youngest son's effeminacy, her daughter's promiscuity, and her eldest son's upcoming parole hearing but otherwise offered no complaints. Inspired both by Mr. Gibson and Dr. Cringen Midlin unleashed all the fury of preventive medicine on her, beginning with a pap smear, mammogram, and colonoscopy and ending with prescriptions for estrogen, aspirin, and Zoloft. Mr. Lawrence was next, and at first thwarted Midlin's zeal for action with up-to-date cholesterol, blood sugar, prostate examination, and colonoscopy reports. Midlin was able to resume his crusade, though, for Mr. Lawrence's eyes misted tellingly when he spoke of his deceased wife and he was promptly given aspirin and Zoloft. Next came a relative lull with Mrs. Lewis, who wasn't due for a pap smear, mammogram, or colonoscopy and

---

[7] An unsuccessful assault in which Sir Horatio Nelson lost his right arm.

was already on estrogen, aspirin, and Zoloft. Midlin's next patient, Mr. Stevens, was a perfectly normal and asymptomatic man with no business even being in a clinic. As he left with his aspirin he was slightly confused and wondered if his new prescription signified serious illness. As the last chart on his stack was brought to him Midlin tore his mind away from thoughts of a greasy fried lunch and allowed the name to mentally register. He felt his spirits soar as he recognized a familiar name who could surely benefit from additional preventive practices.

Mr. Bishop was an 80-year-old veteran of the Pacific War who was a favorite of Midlin's. Typical of his cohort he was always courteous, humble and frank and he had a kind tolerance of Midlin's still-clumsy ministrations. He was reluctant to speak of his wartime experiences and even more averse to complaint of any kind. In simply talking to him Midlin himself felt both calmed and reassured and he knew that even Dr. Cringen would agree this was one patient with no need for Zoloft. Midlin could not help but see his similarity to Mr. Gibson's normotensive, normolipemic, and nonsmoking profile, however, and the thought of Mr. Bishop suffering the same debilitating illness horrified him. He resolved that Mr. Bishop would leave with a prescription for aspirin, even though he guessed from previous experience that it would be a hard sell. He broached the subject with a friendly, mock-firm tone he had heard Dr. Cringen use effectively.

"Look, Mr. Bishop, I want you to take an aspirin," he said.

Mr. Bishop looked surprised but seemed willing to comply. "Just one?" he asked.

Midlin blushed a little and laughed. "No, one every day."

"Well, for how long?"

Midlin realized for the first time that he was asking quite a lot when he answered, "Um, for good, for the rest of your life."

Mr. Bishop pondered this with a distasteful expression and

had already begun shaking his head. "Look, I've let you people poke me with needles and put stuff in my behind and I never really saw much point in it. I know a little about that stuff, though, and it's for headaches. My head feels fine."

Midlin laughed to himself at this simplistic but endearing approach and felt he was on firmer ground. "No, this is a different dose and is for stroke and heart attack prevention, not headaches."

The battle was protracted, with Mr. Bishop arguing his side with the facts that he felt fine, was on a tight budget, and had never taken a medication in his life. Midlin countered with citation of the medical literature and appeals to Mr. Bishop's personal and family responsibilities with ultimate success. As he handed Mr. Bishop the prescription he breathed a sigh of relief and said, "Thanks for doing this, Mr. Bishop, it's dangerous for you not to."

Mr. Bishop looked from Midlin's eyes to the floor and back and said softly, "You know I've been shot at, don't you, son?"

CHAPTER 11

Tees was extremely agitated today. Midlin was surprised by this, for although agitation was certainly typical in Tees, this day of all days Midlin thought Tees would have learned to control himself. Instead, he was manifesting even more of the very energy, agitation, and belligerence that had landed him in a hell of personal meetings and notes in his permanent record all the day before. Far from cowed, Tees was apparently responding with redoubled efforts to both expose the fallacies and belittle the mission of modern medicine. Midlin still had not worked with Flynn but had heard enough of him through his colleagues to see that Tees was in large part inspired by Flynn's tutelage. The eternal pessimism in patient outcomes coupled with biting sarcasm was clearly recognizable, and in Tees' case this was coupled with a tense, tooth-grinding energy that was overtly confrontational.

The trouble had really begun long before Tees'

decompensation the other day, for Mrs. Eubens had been Tees' special charge ever since her admission on his first day on call in the ICU. This shapeless, 400-pound morass had been found unresponsive on her couch by her daughter and the paramedics had been summoned from a pay phone near her trailer park. This had represented a marked change in Mrs. Eubens' condition, for she had lain minimally responsive on the couch for the last several years. Her daughter, far from svelt herself, had enabled Mrs. Eubens' propensity for sloth with constant attention that included cheeseburgers, cheesecakes, and bedpans. The paramedics had been forced to borrow a chainsaw from a nearby wrecking yard and extricate Mrs. Eubens through a massive hole in her trailer wall. Four of them had then been required to place her on two gurneys in the back of the ambulance. In the emergency room she had been severely hypotensive (as best as could be determined through inches of fat by a blood pressure cuff designed for the thigh but placed on her arm) and when the rotten, gangrenous bedsores covering her entire left side had been discovered she had been declared "septic." This catchphrase denotes a patient suffering a low blood pressure due to the systemic presence of bacterial byproducts. These products cause a diffuse dilation of the peripheral arterioles with circulatory collapse as well as causing a massive release of the inflammatory mediators with which the ICU staff was so painfully familiar. Mrs. Eubens had been intubated on the spot, and a surgical incision had been required for the placement of an extra-long venous catheter through which a large volume resuscitation was then performed. Tees had then greeted her at the doors of the ICU and had escorted her, five nurses, two respiratory technicians, three transporters and a resident to the room where she had lain for the next twenty-five days. Tees, as the intern on call that day, had been primarily responsible for Mrs. Eubens' management and paperwork for the duration of her stay.

Every aspect of caring for Mrs. Eubens had been difficult. It had been almost impossible to place the requisite tubes in her many hidden orifices, and once they were in place every effort had been made to maintain them. Her constant gelatinous jiggling had made this difficult, however, as had the double-sized bed with variable inflation which had raised and lowered her like a boat on the tide, constantly redistributing her weight to prevent the formation of new bedsores. Stethoscopes had yielded no noise when applied to her chest, and the cherished physical exam technique of percussion had only worsened the unmanageable jiggling. When Mrs. Eubens had developed the characteristic ICU complication of gastric ulcers and bleeding there had therefore been no warning until globs of sticky, reddish-brown stool bubbled up from between her legs. A common ICU complication resulting from stress-induced gastric acid secretion and mucosal sloughing, Mrs. Eubens' bleeding had been so severe that a surgical incision through the two-foot thick layer of blubber on her abdomen had been required to remove a part of her stomach. That incision had yawned widely ever since, doomed from the start not to heal given the lack of proper blood supply in this indolent tissue. Midlin had seen Tees almost disappear while packing gauze into this wound.

Midlin had at first thought that Tees enjoyed having Mrs. Eubens on his service. His reference to both her and her obese daughter as "two peas in a pod" had drawn a laugh from the crowd on rounds, and she had otherwise provided Tees with comic relief in the early days of his ICU rotation. He had wondered, for instance, why Mrs. Eubens' left arm was of relatively normal size. Given the logistics of her existence her left arm should have been trapped immobile beneath her bulk, unable to aid her dominant right arm in its constant quest for cheeseburgers. By all rights, Tees had argued, that left arm should have atrophied like the unused off-claw of a lobster. The arm had somehow maintained itself with the rest of her vast bulk, however, seemingly contrary to the biologic laws of supply and demand. While he seemed to have had little regard for Mrs. Eubens herself, Tees had held her left arm in some esteem.

This idyllic relationship had been doomed to sour, however, and it did so the day Mrs. Eubens' central venous line developed an infection. Needless to say this fact had been discussed on rounds and arrangements for antibiotics, cultures, and more vigorous temperature monitoring had been made. Tees had been given the unenviable task of placing a new central venous catheter and Midlin had known enough to make himself scarce all morning, for he had found himself doing Tees' undesirable jobs more than once this year. Midlin had returned from an unnecessary trip to the radiology department in time to see Tees swabbing a vast orange circle of iodine on Mrs. Eubens' vast chest. As he scrubbed in the traditional inside-out spiral Tees had cursed Dr. Seldinger with a truck driver's vocabulary.

The Seldinger technique had revolutionized modern medicine in many ways. This integrated system of needles and wires allows for the placement of a catheter in the large veins of the torso and subsequently provides a large conduit for medication administration or withdrawal of blood. The large volume of blood flowing in these veins dilutes medicines administered through the catheter and so relatively caustic preparations can be infused without the scarring and thrombosis that would accompany peripheral intravenous administration. The faster flow and larger size of the target veins also makes them less susceptible to clot formation, a complication befalling any smaller vein with a catheter left in it. All of the monitoring, blood drawing, fluid resuscitation, and medication administration that the ICU held so dear was therefore completely dependent on the presence of these catheters, and

Tees had therefore been under some pressure as he poised a very long needle over Mrs. Eubens' chest. Her nurses had stood scowling at the side of the room, arms laden with IV bags and syringes and shifting irritably from foot to foot as they waited for a route by which to restore Mrs. Eubens' physiologic equilibrium.

The Seldinger procedure begins with a needle stick into the selected target vessel. The femoral vein of the groin, jugular vein of the neck, or subclavian vein under the collarbone is selected according to a variety of considerations and the overlying skin is painted orange with the traditional iodine solution never yet proven effective. Lidocaine is used to anesthetize the skin, then a three-and-a-half inch needle is advanced into the vein of choice. A syringe attached to the back of the needle is kept at constant negative pressure, and when the tip of the needle enters a vein of that caliber there is an abrupt "flash" of dark blue venous blood that fills the 5cc syringe instantly. Once the needle tip occupies the lumen of the vein a curved, blunt-ended "J" wire is advanced through the needle bore and travels several centimeters along the inside of the chosen vein. The needle can then be removed and a progression of tapered tissue dilators can be passed along the wire, to be followed ultimately by the catheter itself once the way is cleared. Only after the catheter is in place is the wire finally removed, and the catheter is stitched in place with due reverence. The whole process can take as little as ten minutes to complete on a normal individual whose anatomy is discernible to the eye. In a patient like Mrs. Eubens no such landmarks exist, however, making each stab with the needle as wild as a shot from a blunderbuss and with similar destructive capacity. The large veins in these regions are accompanied by large arteries, and in addition there are nearby organs such as the bladder or lungs to contend with. The Seldinger technique can be used to place a catheter in an artery as well, but an artery inadvertently torn by a needle with no subsequent catheter placement to plug the hole can result in life-threatening hemorrhage. A needle in the lung of a patient on positive-pressure ventilation will cause an air leak and lung collapse which also can be life-threatening, especially in Mrs. Eubens as a pneumothorax would be difficult to diagnose in lungs inaudible to stethoscopes and a chest impenetrable to x-rays. Needless to say, Tees had been grinding his teeth even before he had picked up the special-order seven-inch needle and made his first blind pass in the region of Mrs. Eubens' collarbone.

Tees' choice of the subclavian vein had been a matter of pure necessity. Mrs. Eubens' groin was covered by a vast expanse of fat into which both her bladder catheter and rectal tubes seemingly disappeared. Her neck waddle covered a similar extent of real estate and effectively obscured the location of her jugular vein, and so Tees had been left attacking a collarbone he could barely feel. With each pass of the long needle Tees had looked unavailingly at the empty syringe in his hand, then anxiously to the monitor display for reassurance that if the needle wasn't in a vein is was at least not in a lung. The line of nurses waiting to administer medications had begun to grow, and with this nidus an actual crowd of gawkers had eventually gathered. Each had seen a number of catheters placed and each had a special bit of advice for Tees.

"Are you aiming at her sternal notch?" one nurse had asked. Mrs. Eubens' sternal notch could not have been seen by even the most discerning eye.

"Have someone pull on her arm!" another nurse had said, reaching for an arm and upsetting the sterile tray in the process.

"Is there a rolled-up towel under her spine?" a third had asked, viewing the figure before her and deciding not to try to look for herself.

"You have to tap the clavicle with the needle. Are you tapping the clavicle?"

Tees had by this time become covered in sweat and after ten needle passes his efforts had clearly been diminishing in intensity and enthusiasm, but this unsolicited assistance finally caused him to snap. He had dropped all pretense at catheter placement and began to whoop loudly even though somewhat muffled by his sterile mask. He had begun a deliberate dance around the bed making a variety of noises, first bending low to the floor then raising his hands to the sky. He had then stopped and faced the astonished crowd.

"Your advice is appreciated, but I do this three times around the bed before I start. Then I rub myself in garlic, throw salt over my shoulder, pick up a penny, and wish on a shooting star. If all that doesn't do it I don't know how a towel is going to help."

With this Tees had walked from the ICU. No one had spoken to him or had tried to stop him, in fact quite the opposite. The nurses and other staff had shied away and avoided his eye as he had walked by, and he had been gone before Killion arrived to investigate the raindance which had awakened him. Killion, anxious to return to bed and having placed thousands of catheters in his lifetime, had simply opened a new seven-inch needle and had stuck it directly into Mrs. Eubens' subclavian vein. He had been back in his cot nine minutes later.

Tees' stormy relationship with Mrs. Eubens had deteriorated from that point on. Midlin had seen the look of disgust on his face grow more pronounced each day as he tended to her, and the fact that she served as a constant reminder of his catheter placement inadequacies had not improved his attitude toward her. Tees' comments on rounds had gradually evolved from humorous whale references through embittered nastiness to an outright campaign for withdrawal of care. The topic of "pulling the plug" was essentially never discussed in the ICU and Midlin had never seen the topic seriously considered. Tees' initial allusions to his plan for Mrs. Eubens had therefore been ignored with only an occasional smile. The intensity of his campaign had increased, however, until no one had been able to ignore his aggressive commentary on the waste of resources Mrs. Eubens represented. The things Tees said on rounds had spread shock and horror through the staff, and Midlin had experienced shock himself when he realized the accuracy of most of Tees' statements. Tees had eventually generalized his campaign to indict life support efforts throughout the unit and had thereby managed to alienate most of the staff by his third week, but Mrs. Eubens had always been his favorite target and Mrs. Eubens' nurses had hated him the most. Even the nurses with whom Tees had slept had eventually turned on him and vilified him with zeal.

Adding to his unpopularity, Tees had been very hard to argue with on this topic. It had not just been his overbearing and energetic presence but also his absolute conviction and accuracy. There had been no denying the fact that all of Mrs. Eubens was disgusting and half of her was rotting like leftovers at the back of the refrigerator. There had also been no denying the fact that she was accumulating bills at the base rate of over five thousand dollars a day, an expense that would be difficult to justify for even a Nobel laureate. All had been aware that the chance of her paying these bills was infinitesimal, especially given the recent decline in her trailer's resale value. In the last twenty years, in fact, Mrs. Eubens hadn't actually earned enough money to pay for one day of the ICU's attentions. Lastly, it had been clear to all but had been stated only by Tees that Mrs. Eubens would never survive to return to her couch and cheesecakes no matter how much money was spent on her.

Tees' big break with the ICU staff had finally occurred the day before. He had begun a one-dollar, winner-take-all gambling pool in which each contestant attempted to guess Mrs. Eubens' hospital bill. He had cajoled and badgered the generally reluctant staff to enter the event in a manner that had bordered on extortion, and by noon there had been over forty dollars to be won. Tees' recruitment had been less than subtle, however, and a number of visiting patient relatives had witnessed his efforts. They had understandably misinterpreted the activity as betting on Mrs. Eubens' survival and of course the truth had been no more appropriate. Numerous complaints had been lodged with the hospital administration and when the meetings began there had been any number of nurses available to corroborate Tees' inappropriate behavior. With all the commotion Tees had still been able to call the hospital billing office for an up-to-date reckoning on Mrs. Eubens. The fact that she had owed $273,000 had not been considered justification for Tees' foray into unlicensed lottery and he had summarily been dismissed for the day to deliberate his crime. This had only allowed Tees' nightly party to begin a little earlier, and when Midlin had returned home after an afternoon of double duty it had already been in full swing. Midlin was so tired he had fallen asleep in spite of the techno bass beat from next door that had rattled the change on his nightstand.

Now Tees was back at work for morning rounds and had apparently learned nothing from his ordeal. He stood defiantly on his toes, bouncing up and down with his limitless energy and daring all to contradict him. First he went through his established monologues on the prognoses for Mr. James, Mr. Redding, and Mr. Domer, all of whom had lain in the unit unchanged since their arrival. His ranting was initially greeted with embarrassed silence, for it was immediately clear to all that Tees' afternoon would again be occupied with meetings. Midlin wondered if the administration would arrange a whole retreat for Tees alone. Tees seemed to know that his time with this near-captive audience was limited and that this was most likely his last performance, and so at the first opportunity he moved on to the new material provided by last night's ICU admission.

Mr. Wessel had been hit by a truck. His experience was even more cliché than that, however, as he had also just gotten married and won the lottery (a "play again free" ticket rather than a jackpot of millions, but ironic all the same). The truck had hit him squarely at high speed and then had dragged him for some distance, but unfortunately he had demonstrated vital signs just detectable by the paramedics at the scene. He was duly trussed and transported, and when unbundled in the ICU had literally oozed onto his new gurney. Robbins had spent a sleepless night at Mr. Wessel's side, first mopping away blood and bone fragments to find homes for various catheters and then pouring saline and pressurized oxygen through them in an effort to maintain the precarious vital signs he continued to display on the monitors. Mr. Wessel lay in his bed with all his limbs splinted in anatomically impossible positions and with an otherwise generalized formlessness that betrayed the fact that every bone in his body was broken. He had so lost his normal form that the radiologists were still puzzling over his CT scans 6 hours after his arrival. Already an expensive parade of orthopedists, thoracic surgeons, and neurosurgeons had begun to file past him and argue over who got to operate first on what. Mrs. Wessel, still with the glow of a newlywed in spite of her smeared makeup, sat at the bedside with tearful eyes throughout.

Robbins had begun her presentation of the case with the usual description of vital signs, ventilator settings and catheter positions. As dictated by the format for ICU presentations there was little discussion of what had landed Mr. Wessel in the unit or of whether he might ever get out. The consulting specialists joined the group and the conversation further devolved into a scheduling of OR time, with it finally decided that the bleeding in his chest would be evacuated at the bedside and then the bleeding in his head would be drained and staunched in the operating room. Once these relatively emergent procedures were performed the orthopedists would spend the rest of the day plating, screwing, and rodding his fractured spine, pelvis and limbs. All the while Midlin could see Mrs. Wessel peering around the doorway with an expectant look on her face, edging ever closer like a dog fudging the "stay" command, and he could see that the calm and professional manner of the gray-haired, white-coated group before him had filled her with hope. As the discussion went on he began to feel hopeful himself, forgetting for a moment his sense of despair in first viewing Mr. Wessel. It slowly became clear to him that the consultants were dealing with several hundred small problems from intracranial hemorrhage to broken toes and that each of these could be addressed in turn and in isolation, ultimately to return Mr. Wessel to whole. It was a seemingly innocuous question from the neurosurgeon that finally allowed Tees to interrupt both the proceedings and Midlin's reverie.

"What was this guy's PT on arrival?" the neurosurgeon asked of Robbins. This was a standard measure of clotting ability, used in conjunction with the PTT test. "An elevated PT can be an indicator of brain injury with thromboplastin release and can be a poor prognosticator."

Robbins just had time to respond with "seventeen" before Tees interrupted. He had held his tongue a remarkably long time, but now his frustration and agitation caused his words to tumble forth uncensored. His histrionic outburst took the consultants aback, for they had not been present to witness Tees' daily scenes. Even those accustomed were shocked at the intensity of this, his last performance.

"A poor prognosticator? A poor prognosticator? Jesus Christ, have you been in that room? That guy has massive amounts of intracranial, intrathoracic, and intrapelvic blood and is barely holding his pressure after gallons of transfusion and resuscitation. Every single bone in his body is broken, and that is counting the constituent bones of his skull and pelvis as separate entities. When you poke him he feels like a sack of flour. What do you have to do to be declared dead around here? Get atomized to red mist? My guess is that if anybody here had actually seen the accident they would know this guy is dead already."

Before anyone could react Tees had crossed the few feet to Mrs. Wessel and stood over her. She turned her tearful face up to look at him.

"You saw it, didn't you?" he asked. "A collision of unbelievable force, wasn't it? Don't you know in your heart that your husband is dead, no matter what these people and these monitors tell you?"

Tees never got to hear Mrs. Wessel's response to his interrogation, for Killion was provoked to animated action for the first time that Midlin had ever seen. Killion crossed quickly to Tees and grasped the collar of his white coat, practically picking Tees up off the floor in spite of his height. He then half-carried, half-pushed Tees out the door ahead of him with little ceremony and no apology, and everyone present knew the ICU had seen its last of Tees. Midlin had not witnessed such an exit since the inkwell and pigtail incidents of his grade school days.

The aggregated staff and consultants were left in embarrassed silence with the sobbing Mrs. Wessel. In spite of all Midlin's efforts to the contrary she managed to catch and hold his eye.

"I did see the accident," she said between tearful gasps. "That man is right. My husband is dead, isn't he?"

Midlin took this stranger in his arms and whispered softly so as not to be heard by the others. "Yes," he said. "Yes, he is."

CHAPTER 12

Midlin breathed a sigh of relief as he walked onto the medicine ward for his next month's assignment. His last week in the ICU had been a nightmare of every other night call given Tees' precipitous absence, and Killion's already blunted teaching instinct had been snuffed completely by Tees' outburst. Tees had taken a week of enforced vacation and was back on the job in the ER. He had survived a previous month in the ICU, and so the residency director had declared him eligible for graduation in spite of his lost time. Midlin was now returning to the hectic but familiar world of pneumonia, diabetes, cellulitis, and chronic heart failure and he couldn't have been happier. He would be back under Sargent's supervision with all the attendant gains in knowledge, and he would be on a much more reasonable schedule. Given the number of interns available he would only go sleepless every fourth night, a prospect he viewed as a veritable vacation.

As always in the hospital, Midlin's relief was short-lived. He joined the traditional first-of-the-month intern meeting to receive his call day assignments and exchanged familiar nods with Robbins, Oggler, and Aines. He had just drawn the short straw for the first night on call when in classic "hot potato" fashion the ward admission pager abruptly burst into strident life with a display of "6336." Cursing his luck and whoever invented the pager Midlin phoned the ER to receive news even more unwelcome than a waiting admission. Mr. Bishop, Midlin's patient from the longitudinal clinic, was in the ER with massive hematemesis.

The bloody vomiting had begun with a single, dramatic eructation just as Mr. Bishop was enjoying his morning coffee. The blood covered the entire surface of the breakfast table and Mrs. Bishop had slightly delayed their departure for the hospital in order to tidy up a little. Mr. Bishop's vital signs were perfectly stable on his arrival and he had undergone the uncomfortable placement of a nasogastric tube, assisting the ER physician with a combination of gagging and swallowing. The fluid removed through this tube had looked like a suspension of coffee grounds and had been deemed clotted blood. There was no liquid red blood to suggest active bleeding, and so Mr. Bishop was placed in a side room to await an opening in the endoscopy schedule. Midlin would be responsible for his management when he arrived on the ward, after the gastroenterologists looked in his stomach with a fiberoptic scope and determined the cause of the bleeding. Although the possibilities were endless and included many ominous cancerous diagnoses Midlin was more embarrassed than worried, for he was fairly sure he knew what they would find.

His brief conversation with Mr. Bishop confirmed his worst fears. Mr. Bishop had begun taking his daily aspirin four days ago. The generic, normal-strength aspirin had been the cheapest and thus the obvious brand choice. He took the aspirin as his second act every morning, with the event falling between trips to the bathroom and coffee machine. It had been a recipe for disaster, and the coffee had no doubt acted as gasoline on a barbeque fire. The only question remaining in Midlin's mind when he left the room was what exactly the endoscopy would show. There would either be a diffuse gastritis with blood oozing from the very surface of the stomach or there would be focal ulcers burrowing even to the depth of the arteries supplying the stomach wall, either of which would be the direct result of aspirin. In addition to its antiplatelet effect aspirin is a potent inhibitor of the enzyme cyclo-oxygenase, the action of which results in the production of the infamous inflammatory mediator prostaglandin. With no prostaglandin present the normal inflammatory responses of increased blood flow and white cell congregation are blunted, thus producing aspirin's major therapeutic effect. The tissues of the body are dependent on a low baseline level of prostaglandin to maintain their blood supply, and a small amount of prostaglandin causes routine dilation of small blood vessels while larger concentrations create the swelling associated with illness and injury. Aspirin deprives the body of this normal baseline level of blood flow and can therefore have devastating effects on susceptible organs, namely the stomach and kidneys. The cells of the stomach lining are left like a military salient, unsupplied from behind and attacked by gastric acid from the front. When these starved cells die and slough the deeper tissues of the stomach wall, including arteries, are exposed to the depredations of stomach acid with potentially life-threatening hemorrhage resulting. In very rare cases the ulcer can penetrate the stomach wall with even more disastrous consequences. Mr. Bishop was not apparently suffering from these complications and most likely would need only monitoring and antacid medication on the medicine ward, but in spite of this prognosis Midlin felt guilty and dreaded his upcoming confession as the precipitating factor in Mr. Bishop's hospital admission.

Midlin returned to the wards to join rounds, already now in progress. It was never hard to find the doctors on rounds—the large, loud group of white coats was easily tracked down as it moved from room to room every morning. The group consisted of one attending physician, two residents, and four interns and managed up to eighty patients at a time. The group visited every patient every day, the discussion beginning outside the room and then progressing inside to include the patient. Each intern was expected to arrive early enough to see every patient under his care, acquiring data and exam findings to later proffer for analysis by the residents and attending. It was in these sessions that the majority of treatment decisions were made, and it was also here that most teaching and "pimping" took place. Midlin approached the group and surreptitiously joined the circle, causing no commotion as such comings and goings were typical of rounds. The demands of patient care rarely conformed to the educational schedule, and everyone expected the constant interruptions of pagers, nurses, and other noisome pests.

Sargent would be the attending this month. A chief resident in internal medicine is generally a board-certified graduate of the training program who has agreed to accept slave wages for an additional year. The recipients of this coveted position handle resident scheduling and complaints, preside over educational conferences, and also act as attending physicians in the ER and on the medicine wards. The job is considered quite an honor even though it makes little financial sense, and these individuals make very effective teachers given their recent study for the board exams. Sargent, philosophically an echo of the hospital administration, was a typical choice for this role. Flynn, on the other hand, was an unusual choice given his flippancy and Midlin had often wondered what successful act of blackmail had landed him the spot. Flynn was at least generally regarded as an excellent teacher, although Sargent had once characterized their respective styles as "didactic and sarcastic."

Rounds went quickly this morning, for the presentations were handled by the residents on this one day every month. The resident and intern schedules were staggered by one week so that there was a seamless transition of patient care responsibilities, and the residents present today had therefore been on the ward service for the last three weeks. The practiced presentations of the residents excited no comment from Sargent, but the interns knew that after a day of familiarization they would be presenting the cases in a much less supportive atmosphere. This thought made Midlin turn a considering eye toward his fellow interns, against whose performances he would be measured that month. This assessment was performed by every intern coming on service, for most people this far along the educational conveyor belt tend to guard their intellectual reputations zealously. He knew to expect head-shaking uncertainty from Aines and short-sighted meticulousness from Robbins, but he had seen too little of Oggler professionally to draw any conclusions. He hoped Oggler's ability level lay somewhere above competence but somewhere below his own.

Rounds had a traditional ending that morning, with the group coming to rest at the patient with the longest current stay. This unwritten arrangement allowed the busier participants to shed themselves from the group, for rarely were there significant issues to decide in such patients. Midlin was only a little surprised to see Mr. Larkin occupy this honored position. He was now in his fifth month of hospitalization.

Mr. Larkin's face lit up as Midlin entered the room only to darken as he saw Sargent close behind. Once the group introductions were made and discussion began Midlin became quiescent in assuming that Sargent would protect him from a verbal tethering, but when Mr. Larkin suddenly launched on a tale of debauchery he became suspicious. Looking around, he saw that the others had exited stealthily and left him alone with the infirm bard. Deciding to make the best use of his time, Midlin half-listened to a story about the young Mr. Larkin and a much younger soda fountain girl while he surveyed the damage modern medicine had wrought over the past few months.

There were the usual catheters in Mr. Larkin's bladder and veins. Other rubber tubes sprouted elsewhere from his body, mostly in areas where nature had not originally provided orifices. A colonoscopy (unappetizingly performed with the same fiberoptic scope that would soon pass down Mr. Bishop's esophagus) had not provided a definitive diagnosis for Mr. Larkin's vague illness but had most definitively perforated his colon, a complication occurring approximately once every thousand such procedures. There had therefore been a predictable spill of bacteria and vegetable matter that had found its way into every crevice of the peritoneal cavity, a complex cavity housing most of the abdominal organs and thus providing many crevices. Each sequestered stool collection therefore represented a separate focus of infection, with fibrous shaggy walls ultimately developing to isolate each pocket and creating in essence multiple intra-abdominal zits. Each pocket had received the attentions of multiple specialists, with the result that some were drained with catheters placed by radiologists and others were drained with catheters placed by surgeons. Each area was meanwhile bathed in potent intravenous antibiotics prescribed by the infectious disease service. The management of his catheters and medications had completely eclipsed the daily discussions of his care, and most of those involved in his case (including Mr. Larkin himself) had forgotten the circumstances of his initial admission.

Satisfied that the catheter sites and Mr. Larkin looked relatively healthy Midlin excused himself abruptly when Mr. Larkin paused for breath, but of course the last half of the graphic story followed Midlin down the hall. For all the trouble Mr. Larkin could be Midlin discovered he had missed the colorful old guy and he wondered who Mr. Larkin would talk to when he finished his own three-year training.

He returned to the nurses' station to join the other interns in chart review. There was never enough counter space in these areas as there is always an escalation in medical paperwork in the time between designing and building a hospital. In his short career Midlin felt he had already seen a doubling of paperwork, and just as with the accumulation of taxes this burden never showed a decrease. Midlin therefore could not join his colleagues at the table designated for the purpose and was instead forced to pull a chair up to the main counter. Here he struggled to claim space between the massive unit clerk on one side and a spindly priest on the other, and he received intimidating and obsequious glances from each respective quarter. He found himself unable to work as he was progressively encroached upon by Geraldine's bulk and pressed against Father Michael, who seemed rather disconcertingly to welcome the personal contact. He was relieved when Mr. Bishop's gurney arrived from the endoscopy suite and his pager sounded soon thereafter, heralding the endoscopy report from the gastroenterologist. Thankfully Midlin rose, straightened his wrinkled coat, and called the number on his pager display.

The voice on the other end of the line was clearly anxious to return to the profitable occupation of endoscopy.

"That was the easiest diagnosis we've ever had. The guy had four ulcers on the greater curvature, each one the size of an aspirin and all in different stages of healing. The newest one was oozing a little, but there was nothing we needed to coagulate."

Midlin thanked the gastroenterologist and hung up, glad that things hadn't been worse. There had been no need to electrically cauterize a bleeding vessel, and so Mr. Bishop's prognosis was indeed excellent. He would spend a couple nights in the hospital with his nasogastric tube hooked to suction to monitor his stomach for blood and antacid medication to allow his stomach lining to heal. He would not be allowed to eat for most of that time and would instead receive infinitely less satisfying intravenous hydration. Two pints of donated blood would be matched to his type and held in reserve should any setbacks occur or any blood appear in the suction container. Probably the most effective measure in his treatment regimen, however, would simply be the discontinuation of his unnecessary daily aspirin.

Midlin watched as the transporters installed Mr. Bishop in the room next to Mr. Larkin and he was struck by the fact that the two men demonstrated the spectrum of his medical inadequacies from his inability to diagnose to his ability to overtreat. He could start running past the entrances of both rooms in his embarrassment and so the arrangement was at least efficient. One look at Mr. Bishop as he was rolled by told Midlin that their discussion of the endoscopy results would have to be postponed, for Mr. Bishop remained heavily sedated and would not soon be able to converse, operate heavy machinery, or enter into binding legal agreements. This was necessary for endoscopy as the passage of a hose through the gullet was rarely well tolerated by a conscious individual, and as Mr. Bishop clearly had no plans for the remainder of the day the endoscopy nurses had known no restraint in their administration of hypnotics. Mr. Bishop would awaken more completely later in the afternoon with no recollection of the tearful gagging misery he had endured, and he would even ask his nurse when the procedure would begin. With no current prospects of speaking with Mr. Bishop Midlin turned back to his space at the counter, now completely occupied with Geraldine's bulk.

Midlin was reluctant to ask for his place, for he worried that any comment he made would be misconstrued as mockery of Geraldine's size. The hospital had settled a lawsuit with Geraldine's predecessor over much the same sort of thing (the lawsuit had been for harassment, although obviously not sexual). What was more, Midlin had sufficient experience to know he could not afford to antagonize the unit clerk staff. These glorified receptionists were responsible for transcribing doctor's orders as well as distributing paperwork to the far reaches of the hospital. With barely more education than the man who ran the floor buffer a unit clerk could determine whether a doctor's order was implemented immediately, later that day, or not at all. Alienating Geraldine would therefore be as unwise a career move as impregnating the hospital administrator's daughter.

Midlin instead decided to return to the intern's charting table, insinuating himself next to the less sensitive and litigious bulk of Oggler. Here he concentrated on writing admission orders, regulating with strokes of his pen every aspect of Mr. Bishop's existence. The timing and dosage of antacid medications, restrictions on eating and activity, regular blood draws for repeated laboratory values unlikely to change, and meticulous recording and analysis of urine, fecal and nasogastric outputs were provided for. Midlin had reached the bottom of the sheet and was putting the finishing touches on the "as needed" medication orders when he was knocked from his chair by a sudden explosion of activity from Oggler, who jumped from his seat and began running down the hall after a man in a suit. The pharmaceutical representative had arrived, and by Oggler's reaction Midlin knew it must be lunchtime.

Midlin hurried down the hall after Oggler, joined on all sides by the ward interns and residents as they headed for the conference room. Pharmaceutical representatives came to the hospital almost daily, their main function being the transportation of food from a local restaurant to the conference room. Ostensibly, the representatives came to present new products or new uses for old products, usually citing corporate-sponsored clinical trials as justification for the use of their expensive offerings. In practice, most representatives gave a 30-second speech which was usually drowned by the chatter of the milling house officers as they gathered their free lunches and picked through the party favors laid out on various tables. There were pens, notepads, EKG calipers, reference books and cards, and even an occasional stethoscope all bearing brand names and allowing for the hospital-wide display of pharmaceutical logos. These items were snapped up eagerly by the impoverished interns with little or no concern for their origins or for the attendant increases in drug costs they precipitated. A walk through the medicine wards could resemble a drive through the town's outskirts, with logos flashing by like billboards on a highway. The excitement of these fledgling doctors must have struck the representatives as humorous, for purchasing the loyalty of attending physicians required the much more extreme offerings of vacation cruises or cash.

Today's short, almost inaudible presentation centered on the diuretic drug Lasix. This is a proprietary version of the generic drug furosemide, and as with almost all drugs there is no discernable difference in the action of the two preparations. Today's representative used words such as "familiarity" and "universality" to justify the use of Lasix, no doubt in an effort to capitalize on effective marketing by past representatives. It certainly is true that the brand name Lasix is in widespread use throughout the country's hospitals, having replaced the term furosemide much like 'Kleenex' has come to mean a facial tissue. In keeping with this analogy the use of Lasix rather than furosemide is far more costly, amounting to many dollars per dose. For a drug administered up to four times a day this amounts to a massive expenditure, enough to keep the country's interns in pens and notepads for eternity. While any doctor asked to describe the difference between a generic and a brand name preparation will immediately allow that no therapeutic difference exists, when the time comes to order a diuretic drug most will simply write "Lasix" without a second thought. Aware of the power of this name recognition most pharmaceutical presenters aspired to a simple repetition of the brand name with no real underlying substance. Midlin ate his lunch to a chorus of "Lasix, Lasix, Lasix" in one ear and Oggler's exaggerated chomping in the other and was reminded of the adage that no lunch was really free.

His return to the ward coincided with a scene of great chaos and activity centered outside the rooms of Mr. Larkin and Mr. Bishop. Whoever was the subject of concern, thought Midlin, it would be up to him to respond and also could very well be his fault. As he neared the scene he heard the word "seizure" spoken by several of the nurses, and this at least calmed his fears somewhat.

A seizure, of course, can be a life-threatening event. The smoothly ordered, precise electrical impulses normally coursing through the brain have become disordered and erratic, skipping about the cortex with no adherence to established neuronal pathways. The typical consequences include jerking and flailing of the limbs, involving one or all extremities depending on the extent of brain involved. Death can result from this disordered contraction as the muscles involved in respiration can also be affected. Most seizures involve complete loss of consciousness, involuntary emptying of the bladder and bowels, and later inability to recall the episode. In addition, most patients suffer a profound somnolence after the seizure that can take hours to resolve. Midlin's complacency in the face of these possibilities was the direct result of Sargent's teaching, for she had declared the seizure to be the most overdiagnosed condition in medicine. She had even gone so far as to declare herself a "seizure cynic," always suspecting a different condition as the underlying cause. There are any number of abnormalities that can result in spasmodic limb movements from fainting spells to delirium tremens, and while nurses and paramedics often reported "seizure activity" this was in fact rarely the case.

Midlin therefore entered Mr. Bishop's room rather calmly, for it was here that the chaotic activity was indeed centered. The nurses, according to their own memorized algorithm, were busily collecting vital signs as he arrived. Mr. Bishop lay on his bed, not jerking but rather contorted and frozen in place. His eyes, still somewhat glazed from his recent sedation, were open and displayed enough emotion to show that he was conscious, scared, and obviously not seizing. Midlin had time to thank Sargent silently, for yet again her teaching had prepared him amply. Midlin allowed his eyes to range over the normal vital signs on the monitors before he stepped just outside the room to confer with Mr. Bishop's attractive primary nurse.

"How did this start?" he asked her, trying to look her in the eyes rather than at her more comely attributes.

"It started right after I gave him his phenergan," she said, having no trouble looking Midlin in the eyes.

"What are you talking about? This guy should only be getting IV ranitidine. I didn't write for anything else."

The nurse defensively grabbed Mr. Bishop's chart and held it under Midlin's nose, effectively blocking his view of her. Midlin was forced to concentrate on the chart itself.

A medication prescribed for a foreseeable but benign patient complaint such as pain, sleeplessness, or nausea is written with the suffix "PRN," an abbreviation for the Latin pro re nata or "as needed." Such a medication is not to be administered regularly but rather only on the request of the patient. As

Midlin scanned his order form he saw that these critical letters were not included, and so the unnecessary medication had been administered right on schedule without a request from Mr. Bishop. As he thought back he realized that his writing had coincided with Oggler's dash to the conference room and, distracted, he had forgotten to add "PRN" to the phenergan order.

Myriad options exist for the treatment of nausea. Possibilities range from the relatively benign antihistamines to the abusable benzodiazepines with which Mr. Bishop was already familiar, with almost every class of drug in between represented in some way. There are very few drugs made specifically for nausea, and most pharmaceuticals utilized for this complaint simply act by sedating the unfortunate sufferer. Phenergan, a drug of the neuroleptic/antipsychotic class, was no exception to this rule. It was in fact an older treatment used to still the delusional rantings of schizophrenics, who once medicated and coherent complained of such sedation as to suggest this alternative use for the drug. Although again the pharmacological options for nausea are limitless every intern in the hospital used phenergan as a PRN drug for nausea, and Midlin on his arrival to this training program had simply followed suit. His one deviation from the norm had been to change his preferred route of administration from rectal to IV following the refusal of a vomiting homophobe. This widespread use of the medication was almost certainly the result of a "phenergan, phenergan, phenergan" presentation by an exuberant pharmaceutical representative at some past lunch conference. It was now clear to Midlin that Mr. Bishop was suffering from a dystonic reaction, a well described but rare complication of the treatment of schizophrenia. The treatment, of course, would involve another medication.

Midlin wrote an order for the effective antidote, careful to write NOW at the end of the line to avoid any confusion. He explained the situation to the nurse, who was relieved for once not to be blamed for a doctor's mistake. She lowered the chart and allowed Midlin a good look.

"You know," she said, "he asked what the medicine was for as I gave it to him and I said 'nausea.' His last words were 'but I'm not nauseated.'"

Midlin laughed in spite of his internal misery. He dreaded even more his upcoming conversation with Mr. Bishop in which he would now confess to the administration of two unnecessary medications, both with disastrous consequences. With his casual medication orders he had twice almost succeeded where the pilots of the Japanese carrier *Akagi* had failed. He spent the remainder of the afternoon canceling all of his previously thoughtless PRN phenergan orders and considered canceling every aspirin prescription he had written in the Longitudinal Care Clinic.

CHAPTER 13

The ward team was once again and as always on rounds. Oggler had been on call the night before and was therefore on the hot seat. In turn he presented each of last night's admissions to Sargent in the traditional format, beginning with History of the Present Illness (HPI) and progressing through allergies, medications, Past Medical History (PMH), Physical Exam (PE), and laboratory values. With constant interruptions and corrections from Sargent it was often difficult to stay within this format but Oggler did so less well than most. For that matter even Aines showed less tendency to become flustered, which certainly put Oggler at the bottom of the pile. Following the objective presentations Sargent would then lead the group in a discussion of differential diagnosis, a list of possible pathologic conditions that could account for each patient's constellation of symptoms and findings. Such a list of possibilities could even be generated in a "classic" or straightforward presentation, making this the favorite game of internists in general and Sargent in particular. Oggler's offerings in this activity were pathetic and he was berated repeatedly for his shortcomings: when the diagnosis was pneumonia Sargent wanted to hear a list of additional possibilities such as asthmatic mucus plug with distal atelectasis, bronchoalveolar cell carcinoma, tuberculosis infection, laryngeal papillomatosis, aspirated foreign body, or of course mummy-handler's pneumonitis. Instead she was forced to listen to mumbling and stalling and ultimately simply recited the differential lists herself. Midlin did feel he learned something from rounds in spite of all the wasted time, however. Oggler was an idiot. Every medical school class fields a rogue, a slut, and a brain but Midlin thought Oggler must have played the two roles of fat guy and fool in his class at Harvard. Midlin's initial mental matchmaking of the two rotund doctors would obviously and disappointingly never come to pass.

Oggler had admitted one patient on whom even Sargent had little to say. Mrs. Carter had been diagnosed with Chronic Myelogenous Leukemia some five years previously and had opted to pursue alternative therapies of her own choosing rather than the recommended courses of chemotherapy that had been offered her. CML is one of many types of leukemia, a kind of cancer arising in the bone marrow. This tumor is facetiously referred to as a "liquid" cancer, for while most tumors cause an identifiable mass that can be targeted with surgery or radiation leukemic tumor cells enter the bloodstream and circulate freely throughout the body. The tumor cells can proliferate to such an extent that they can plug blood vessels with disastrous consequences or crowd the normal cells out of the bone marrow cavities, resulting in anemia, bleeding, and infections. CML is a particularly difficult disease to treat, and the survival statistics he had seen made Midlin wonder if perhaps Mrs. Carter had made the correct choice of non-doctor. Most patients live relatively normal asymptomatic lives following diagnosis only to abruptly deteriorate at some point years in the future when the tumor cells undergo further regression to “blast” or immature forms. This “blast off” phenomenon is usually followed by the development of symptoms and relatively rapid death.

As Mrs. Carter already had an established diagnosis Sargent had little inclination to play her differential diagnosis game. The ward team was relatively glum when entering her room as they were all aware of her prognosis, but a surprisingly cheerful Mrs. Carter greeted them and engaged them in animated conversation. Her husband was silent and sober in the corner of the room, clearly indicating that he at least understood what the future held. It was he who had ultimately insisted on Mrs. Carter’s return to the allopathic medical system when she developed fatigue and persistent infections, and when her local physician had soiled his pants on examination of her blood smear her husband had trundled her off to the hospital to prevent her escape.

Showing none of the embarrassment that Midlin would have thought proper for her circumstances, Mrs. Carter described the treatments she had received over the years. These ran the gamut from expensive but harmless to downright ludicrous and included such inert substances as laetrile, echinacea, and golden seal root. In addition, she had received acupuncture, high colonics, therapeutic massage, and aromatherapy (most of which, incredibly, had been covered by her medical insurance). There had even been a trip to the Far East, during which sex with a renowned shaman had featured prominently. She displayed the bottles of a number of preparations she was currently taking on her mobile patient tray, describing them as “potent” remedies. She attributed her relatively good health over the last several years to these various pursuits and considered her grossly abnormal, blast-filled blood smear to be a mere setback.

At her insistence, Midlin and Oggler began perusing the labels of these preparations. Sargent was clearly unwilling to endorse these "medications" even to this extent and rather rudely interrupted Mrs. Carter's impassioned descriptions of her previous treatments and their efficacy. While Sargent discussed the upcoming chemotherapy treatments with Mrs. Carter, Midlin read such ingredients as "ground pig pituitary gland" and "shark trachea extract" on the bottle labels. The price tag on one small bottle read $350.00.

As they left the room Oggler was predictably ready with a food analogy.

"Imagine," he said, "it's been illegal to put that stuff in sausages for the last hundred years yet she pays $350.00 for a small bottle."

Oggler's comment was all the more appropriate considering the fact that all these pills could amount to was a small protein meal. These biologic compounds would be immediately digested into their constituent molecules and could not possibly have a significant effect, and for that matter pig pituitary or shark trachea molecules have never been shown to have any physiologic action when intact. For this same reason no "insulin pill" exists as the insulin molecule is also a protein and would not survive a trip through the stomach intact. At least Mrs. Carter had gotten a little something for her money by purchasing these and not homeopathic preparations, for homeopathic "medications" contain only water no matter how impressive the labels may appear.

The rounding ward team came to rest at Mr. Bishop's door. Mr. Bishop had been very tolerant of his mismanagement, and Sargent had been kind in not calling attention to the fact that his phenergan administration had been accidental. Midlin was grateful and thought that had Oggler made a similar error no such consideration would have been afforded him. Mr. Bishop had, of course, begun refusing all medications (including the intravenous antacid) following the resolution of his dystonic reaction. It had been mutually agreed, however, that he would spend an extra night in the hospital for observation. His vital signs had remained stable, he had tolerated bland meals of Jell-O, and no blood had appeared in his continuous nasogastric aspirate. In spite of Midlin's efforts to the contrary Mr. Bishop was clearly on the mend.

The group began to file into the room but drew up short, with Midlin bouncing off Oggler's rounded backside. He craned his neck to see what had created the bottleneck and saw Father Michael standing over the bed, murmuring softly and resting one hand on Mr. Bishop's forehead. As Sargent fumed and fidgeted at this delay Father Michael placed a communion wafer on Mr. Bishop's tongue and made the sign of the cross. The spindly priest then began gathering his many icons and looked up to meet Sargent's eye. The glance they exchanged clearly showed that they had had words before this.

"Sorry for holding you up, Dr. Sargent," said the priest with an impish smile. "Mr. Bishop requested some assistance that would work."

Sargent snorted derisively. "If that were true, you would have admitted all these patients to a church and we'd be coming in at the last minute."

Father Michael realized that this was the wrong argument at the wrong time with the wrong doctor and he silently slipped past the group in the entryway, brushing against Midlin as he did so. As Midlin listened to Sargent discuss the details of Mr. Bishop's upcoming discharge he watched the fragments of Mr. Bishop's communion wafer drop into the nasogastric suction container, whisked from the depths of his stomach within seconds of their being swallowed. He couldn't help but wonder if ingestion or complete digestion of the host were required to cleanse Mr. Bishop's soul.

While they were still in the room the admission pager, now clipped to Robbins' insubstantial waistline, began sounding and Robbins quietly slipped from the room to tend to her first admission of the day. She rejoined them as they finished with Mr. Bishop with a distressed look on her face that Midlin at first failed to notice. He was already completing Mr. Bishop's discharge paperwork in his head and was beginning to wonder if he would see the man in clinic. As kind and as tolerant as Mr. Bishop was Midlin had too high an opinion of his intelligence to believe he would ever again voluntarily submit to Midlin's wanton prescribing. When Midlin finally placed a mental signature on the discharge orders he looked to Robbins' face and noted her discomfort, and he thought at first that she must have received notice of a complex admission. Probably some diabetic in heart and renal failure with pneumonia, the kind of patient that would take a meticulous doctor like Robbins several hours to "tuck in." Robbins waited until she had the entire team's attention before she blurted out her news.

"Tees is in the hospital," she said.

At first Midlin thought she simply hadn't known Tees had returned to work. This alone would be enough to upset her, for Tees' behavior had caused the prim and proper Robbins endless discomfort in their month in the ICU together. He quickly realized, however, that Tees must be her new admission. Her distressed attitude was probably due less to concern for Tees' welfare than to her own worries about tending to the volatile intern as a patient. Midlin first debated whether her meticulous approach to medicine would inspire her to perform a rectal and testicular exam on her fellow intern. Only then did he wonder what illness had befallen Tees.

Tees had come to the ER with a WHOML, a beloved acronym which stood for "worst headache of my life." To present with this complaint was essentially to demand that the ER physician order a CT scan of the head followed by performance of a lumbar puncture or "spinal tap." The abrupt onset of a WHOML, usually in the setting of heavy lifting, sex, or a large bowel movement, is the classic presentation of a subarachnoid hemorrhage. Bleeding occurring within the skull is compartmentalized into intraparenchymal, subarachnoid, subdural, or epidural hemorrhage with each type related to a different mechanism of injury and implying a different prognosis. A subarachnoid hemorrhage (SAH) can result from a number of insults from trauma to hypertension but the classic cause is rupture of an arterial "berry" aneurysm. Weak points in the walls of the cerebral arteries allow small bulges to appear in these high-pressure vessels, and these bulges can burst with any transient increase in intracranial blood pressure. Most such aneurysms are present from birth and the tendency to form them frequently runs in families. The blood trapped in the linings of the brain causes severe irritation and results in neck stiffness, photophobia[8], and, of course, a WHOML.

The search for intracranial hemorrhage is a constant but frustrating mission for the emergency room physician. Much like a racing dog and his quest for the electric bunny, ER doctors spend their days ordering head CTs and performing lumbar punctures in a fruitless search for subarachnoid hemorrhage in every WHOML. The amount of blood can be so small that 5% of such hemorrhages can be invisible on even the most sophisticated imaging studies, and this fact necessitates the performance of a lumbar puncture to examine the cerebrospinal fluid for minute amounts of blood. This elusive nature of SAH coupled with the fact that many other disorders can also result in the complaint of WHOML (meningitis, migraine headache, tension headache, cluster headache, and temporal arteritis to name just a few) means that only one out of every thousand head CT scans for WHOML actually

[8] Extreme sensitivity to light.

demonstrates a subarachnoid hemorrhage. Adding to this futility is the fact that surgery or other specific therapy for SAH is rarely performed, and patients will either die or recover depending on the location and amount of hemorrhage regardless of the efforts of the medical establishment. The identification of SAH therefore only results in more expensive testing in pursuit of an underlying berry aneurysm, which can then be treated expensively to prevent further episodes of bleeding.

Tees had not been lifting, on the toilet, or having sex when his WHOML began (Midlin found this last somewhat incredible). He had come through the back door of the ER and thus was in the CT scanner within half and hour, having circumvented the fumblings of the triage nurse at the front desk and thus avoiding several hours of waiting and several stacks of forms. He was fortunate that the radiologist was sufficiently caffeinated and alert to identify a small amount of subarachnoid blood in his brain, and so he was spared a spinal skewering with a three-and-a-half-inch needle. Immediately upon diagnosing this disorder the ER staff did…nothing. Tees received some pain medication and his admission for observation was arranged. This assured that if a second bleeding episode occurred his death by seizure or stroke could be witnessed by medical personnel. Seizure could result from irritation of the brain's meningeal coverings while stroke could occur due to spasm of irritated vessels. Although no effective therapy exists for this "vasospasm" Tees' observation period would last up to a week to cover the window of time in which this complication can occur, again to make certain the episode would be witnessed. It only remained for Robbins to arrange Tees' cerebral angiogram with the interventional radiology service.

Interventional radiology is a specialty that has come into being due to the efforts of Dr. Seldinger, for his technique of wire-guided catheter placement has been expanded to allow placement of a catheter at the origin of almost any vessel in the body. A vast array of wires of different lengths and varied kinks has been developed, and under guidance of an x-ray camera such wires can be placed within the specific vessel of interest. A catheter is then advanced over the wire and the wire removed, just as in the placement of a central venous catheter. The catheter is then attached to a syringe or injection machine and repeated x-rays taken, timed with the injection of a dense iodine-based contrast material that outlines the branches of the injected vessel. For a cerebral angiogram this process is repeated in all four vessels supplying the brain, and a similar application of the technique can be used for the coronary vessels supplying the heart, the renal arteries supplying the kidneys, or the femoral arteries supplying the legs. The starting point is the same no matter what the organ of ultimate interest, for the femoral artery provides a palpable, accessible portal to the vascular system that no interventionalist can resist.

Midlin did not envy Tees' predicament. Obviously to have a WHOML from SAH is not pleasant, but Midlin's concern for Tees centered on the potential complications of an angiogram. The wires and catheters snaking through the vascular system can dislodge atherosclerotic plaque or form clot on their tips, allowing for distal embolization and stroke. The contrast material can cause renal failure, allergic reactions, and hypotension, any of which can be life-threatening. Lastly, the needle puncture of the femoral artery can result in massive bleeding which can dissect up the retroperitoneal space and remain invisible to the eye of an examiner. While these complications are rare they are for the most part unpredictable and independent of the ability of the interventionalist, making the procedure a veritable crap shoot (although at better odds than Vegas offers). Midlin felt for Tees and was worried about the angiogram. Tees was already unlucky enough to have had a subarachnoid hemorrhage, and so further risk-taking of any kind seemed unwise.

It was not until later that day and after the angiogram that Midlin was able to visit Tees. He practically had to wait in line at Tees' door, for whenever a member of the hospital staff was admitted the news spread like wildfire and every person Tees had even nodded to in the hallway felt obligated to wish him well. Even a few of the nurses Tees had infuriated came to visit, apparently with no hard feelings, and Midlin saw them sizing each other up and assessing the competition for Tees' future affections. Tees remained somewhat sedated from his pain medication and from the hypnotics used for the procedure, but this was fortunate as it made his present situation more bearable. Tees had to lie perfectly flat for at least four hours, otherwise the contraction of his psoas muscle (the tenderloin in cows and pigs) could bounce his perforated femoral artery and start it bleeding. In addition, Tees had been subjected to any number of socially compromising situations that day which had included lying bare-assed naked on a steel table in front of numerous coworkers. His greatest humiliation of all had been the testicular and prostate exams performed by Robbins, who could not be dissuaded to vary from her routine even though Tees' problem was far removed from his perineum. Sargent would heartily approve of her thoroughness the next morning on rounds.

Midlin was initially surprised to hear that the angiogram had shown no abnormality. He was quickly brought up to speed by Sargent, who as always was familiar with the nuances of management of even this relatively rare disorder. The many twists and turns of the cerebral vessels can easily obscure the presence of an aneurysm, especially as these aneurysms are often measured in millimeters. An algorithmic approach to this problem had already been developed, and the correct response to a normal angiogram was simply to perform another angiogram. Thereafter the community coffers receive a much-needed break, for a third angiogram does not statistically increase the chances of finding an elusive outpouching. Subarachnoid hemorrhage and the subsequent two angiograms therefore only supply the interventional staff with leased Mercedes and only provide their offspring with state school educations. Midlin refrained from comment to Sargent, for with this expensive algorithm firmly ensconced in the medical literature and with her Baptist attitude of strict interpretation Midlin knew she would not tolerate questioning on the wisdom of this approach.

It was with great relief that Robbins discharged Tees a week later. He had sailed through his observation period with no evidence of complications and with more visitors than any patient in the history of the hospital. While he had suffered Robbins' ministrations gracefully in the earlier portion of his hospital stay (mostly due to sedation) he had become increasingly more irritable as time went on, becoming ever more like himself with each passing day. Robbins had insisted on a thorough neurological examination every day, poking him with pins, oscillating him with a tuning fork, wiggling his toes up and down and forcing him to walk with bizarre gaits as she vainly searched for the unlikely appearance of a neurologic deficit of which Tees himself was unaware. Tees had finally discovered that opening his hospital gown when she came in the room did deter her somewhat, an act which bothered him little as his modesty had already been so compromised. This and his constant mockery of Robbins' pointless examinations had finally brought him some peace and privacy. For some unfathomable reason Robbins did still insist on a daily auscultation of his heart and lungs, which had always been normal.

Tees was discharged to recover further at home. Investigation into internship regulations had revealed that he was allowed to miss up to three weeks of work for medical reasons and still graduate from his internship. The plan was for him to recover for a week, undergo a second angiogram, recover for another week, and then return to work to finish the year. With just over six months to go Tees would have used up all of his allowable sick time and vacation, and so while still possible his successful completion of internship would require both optimal behavior and health. Midlin thought this graduation highly unlikely when he returned home that night to hear the same music, voices, and bustle emanate from Tees' apartment with even more vigor than usual.

CHAPTER 14

Sargent began their last rounds together by pointing at Midlin, and he mentally prepared his most recently memorized lists for recitation in response to an anticipated question. Instead no question was forthcoming, only a statement that left Midlin wondering as to her seriousness.

"Remember Mr. Morgan?" she asked, forcing Midlin to search back in his memory some four months to recall the pneumonia patient who had been his first intubation. Sargent gave him a second to nod and then continued. "I got some test results yesterday. He had Legionella pneumonia."

Midlin was absolutely shocked. Not because Mr. Morgan had had the relatively rare infection first described at a Legionnaire's convention in Philadelphia and not because Sargent was again demonstrating her thoroughness but rather because he couldn't believe at this point that anyone could possibly care. Mr. Morgan had been discharged from the hospital three months ago and had played approximately forty rounds of golf since that time without a single symptom, yet here was Sargent imparting the results of a five-hundred dollar test that had been mailed out as it was only performed in a limited number of labs in the country. Mr. Morgan's antibiotic coverage for his pneumonia had included drugs that were effective against this infection, making specific expensive testing such as this all the more unnecessary. As always Midlin did not voice these thoughts, for he could see the enormous satisfaction on Sargent's face and also noted something like hero-worship on Robbins'. Oggler and Aines didn't seem to care, and Midlin thought that Mr. Morgan would be unconcerned as well. $500 could buy a lot of golf.

The remainder of rounds that day was similar, for Sargent was in rare form. The discussion of every patient on rounds was taken to new heights. Attention was paid to every last detail that had previously seemed innocuous, tests were ordered for conditions thought already to be diagnosed, and medications were prescribed for every last complaint the patients voiced. At first Midlin didn't understand, for he had thought that Sargent was always performing at the height of precision and vigilance with no room for improvement. As they walked past the nurses' station for the fifth time that morning, a glance at the work schedule for the next month made everything clear to him. Flynn was coming.

Midlin's experience of the last six months had convinced him that most medical documentation was performed in order to impress other doctors. Few people otherwise read medical documentation, and certainly no one else is able to decipher and understand it. Most lawsuits occur in spite of extensive documentation, and in the face of lawyers fluent in doublespeak and juries utterly ignorant of even the simplest medical concepts no amount of documentation can provide a legal defense for what are usually unavoidable outcomes. Midlin had seen innumerable errors in his brief career (his own and those of others) and none had resulted in legal action, while all of the lawsuits of which he was aware (mostly involving the unfortunate patients of the unfortunate Aines) centered on patient deaths or lesser tragedies that even the presence of Osler, Mohammed, or Jesus could not have altered. Documentation was therefore simply a forum in which the author could display his extensive medical knowledge and place his own entry in the game of differential diagnosis. Every intern lived in fear of forgetting some critical element in the standard workup of a complaint, such as the testing of cerebrospinal fluid for syphilis. It was of no importance that Midlin had never seen a patient with tertiary neurosyphilis (a disease in this day and age just slightly less common than smallpox)—if the test were omitted following acquisition of CSF by lumbar puncture another physician was sure to come along and note the oversight, taking the opportunity to demonstrate his own intellectual might and the former's inadequacy. The result was endless testing for rare, untreatable, and often even unheard of disorders at a vast expense to all involved. Given their long history of antipathy Sargent was determined not to be shamed by her nemesis when he arrived to assume leadership of the ward team in the morning, and she applied this principle to every patient on the service that day.

Rounds stretched into the early afternoon that day given Sargent's pathologic drive to diagnose and treat, and by the end the agitation in both Oggler and Aines was reaching feverish intensity. Following rounds each intern is responsible for a progress note on each patient as well as acquisition and analysis of the result of each test or procedure ordered that day. This extension of rounds meant that the two interns would likely miss dinner that night, and while both were clearly upset Oggler appeared almost apoplectic. Midlin was less worried as he was again on call and therefore had all of twenty-four hours to complete his notes in between the day's hospital admissions. Robbins, of course, missed dinner almost every night anyway and so was unconcerned.

Sargent persisted in her aggressive supervision throughout the day and night. In spite of her exalted position as attending physician she clearly had no intention of sleeping that night. Midlin thought she must feel like a CEO whose books and actions would undergo yearly board review the next morning. To make matters worse there was a continuous stream of admissions from the ER that even made Midlin's head whirl despite his familiarity with inhuman workloads. The activity continued well into the night, long after the belated departure of the other interns and long after Midlin's ability to concentrate had departed as well. It was not until midnight that Midlin and Sargent were able to make the traditional pilgrimage to the radiology department to review the night's cases. Most internists and other clinicians made an effort to view these radiologic studies in spite of their inability to interpret the films themselves, and most of the benefit from this process came from consultation with a radiologist.

As they entered the darkened reading room in the deepest bowels of the hospital Midlin instinctively flipped on the lights, an act which was met with screams of pain and horror from the radiology resident on call. Midlin quickly reversed the switch and only after several minutes did the radiologist dare to uncover his eyes and address them. The subtleties of grayscale can be extremely difficult to appreciate even for those performing the task daily, and radiologists depended heavily on dark adaptation by their irises and retinas to perform their jobs correctly. Midlin had committed the radiology equivalent of urinating in the punch bowl.

Mr. Jackson had come to the ER for the second time in a week complaining of shortness of breath and for the second time had received a chest x-ray. He was 45 years old, black, and his work precluded a hospital visit during normal hours. This meant that each x-ray was initially interpreted by the ER physician alone. Often due to workload and logistic difficulties (as well as the traditional laziness and after-hours scarcity of radiologists) an x-ray taken in this setting can sit for hours before being viewed by appropriately trained and dark-adapted eyes. The written report thus generated can take days to wend its way back to the desk of the ordering physician, who by that time has often forgotten who the patient was and why the x-ray was taken. To make matters worse the report is usually in a bizarre and misleading language that only radiologists speak and understand. A tumor can be variably described as a mass, density, nodule, fullness or other nonspecific moniker while unconcerning variants of normal are tagged with such horrific-sounding Latin names as pectus excavatum or corpora amylacea. With this potential for confusion and error it is not surprising that Mr. Jackson was sent on his way after his first chest x-ray and the written report had not been viewed by clinical eyes even by the time he returned to the ER with the same complaint. He had been on the way out the door a second time without diagnosis or medication when a sharp-eyed radiology technologist with a high school education had noted the abnormality on his film.

"We're here to see Jackson's chest x-ray," said Sargent, positioning herself in the usual spot over the resident's shoulder and eliciting excited expostulations from him.

"Jackson, yes yes yes. Great case." He stepped on a foot pedal that set the giant alternator vibrating, bringing forth panel after panel of transilluminated films. Midlin saw necks, abdomens, and feet flash by until the panel with Mr. Jackson's chest settled into place. It looked completely normal to him, and a glance at Sargent told him she was also struggling to see why everyone was so concerned about Mr. Jackson.

The radiologist began pointing at a number of white areas

overlying the heart and great vessels in the center of the chest, and he also pointed to a few places where Midlin saw nothing at all.

"Here. Here. Here. See that? He has mediastinal lymphadenopathy, mostly paratracheal and hilar."

Midlin could see that Sargent was just as uncertain of what she was looking at as he was but she was obviously not willing to display her ignorance by asking questions. She and the radiologist quickly found common ground in a love of lists, however, and so there was plenty to discuss. Each in turn provided a differential possibility with increasing excitement, talking over one another like two foreign travelers discovering they hail from a common hometown. By the end the possibilities ranged from benign nonspecific enlarged lymph nodes through a variety of infections to aggressive cancer that would kill Mr. Jackson by tomorrow morning and Midlin didn't really feel much wiser. Sargent seemed satisfied, however, and they left the department for the light, space, air and logos of the medicine ward.

As they sat at the charting table outside Mr. Jackson's room Midlin took Sargent's dictation and his pen practically smoked. He wrote orders for a CT scan of the chest to better define the size and distribution of enlarged lymph nodes should a biopsy be required. He ordered tests of the skin and sputum for tuberculosis and expensive blood tests for histoplasmosis infection. An even more expensive blood test for sarcoidosis was also added to the list, although in many such cases the test would be negative even in the presence of the disease. Such lymph nodes can also be the result of a tumor, either a primary mediastinal lymphoma or metastatic tumor arising from a renal or colonic tumor and so a CT scan of the abdomen and a colonoscopy were also requested. As Mr. Jackson had reported occasional coughing and his x-ray suggested tuberculosis, however, this was Sargent's primary concern. Such a patient can present a public health risk and so a special hermetically sealed room was prepared for him. Every health care worker entering the room would require a personally fitted mask that imparts a vaguely porcine appearance to the wearer. Serial tests of Mr. Jackson's sputum for the characteristic red-staining bacteria would be required to exclude an infectious state and these precautions would be instituted until such time as his spit was declared harmless. Midlin had just paused to stretch and massage his cramping hand when both his personal pager and the admission pager sounded simultaneously.

Midlin answered his personal pager first, as such summons generally meant a problem with a patient on the ward. Mr. Griggs, a patient of Aines', had developed acute shortness of breath and as Midlin spoke to his nurse he could hear the beeping of monitors in the background which signaled the degree of her concern. Sargent, in a benevolent mood and apparently not as tired as Midlin, offered to handle the incoming admission and freed him to deal with Mr. Griggs. They agreed to meet following discharge of their respective duties.

Such "cross-cover" calls were common for the intern on call, for no intern's orders could cover every overnight eventuality with PRN medications. All the same, the receipt of such a call was generally viewed as a sign of improper management by the responsible intern and Aines would be in Midlin's debt come morning. Cross-cover calls were usually of little importance, generally centering on such patient complaints as the poor quality of dinner or back pain due to the cheap hospital mattresses. As Midlin hurried to Mr. Griggs' room, however, the sight of scurrying nurses and the sound of blood pressure and oximetry monitors suggested that this call would not be dismissed so lightly as most. Midlin sighed as he realized he would lose at least an hour of sleep as he reviewed Mr. Griggs' chart, examined the patient himself, and waited at the nurses' station until the appropriate measures took effect. Interns rarely slept on call and interns like Robbins never did, but all of them entered into call nights hopefully planning on a few fitful hours which events such as this rudely cut into. Midlin was thus unreasonably irritated with both Mr. Griggs and Aines for this deprivation as he reviewed the chart, and he found himself wishing he were called on Robbins' patients more often as hers was the only legible handwriting currently on the medicine service.

Mr. Griggs had come to the hospital ten days ago having developed the classic complaint of chest pain while shoveling his driveway. Angina, or chest pain brought on by exertion, is due to a progressive narrowing of the coronary arteries and a subsequent gradual diminishment of blood flow to the muscle of the left ventricle. Shoveling snow is a common precipitant, for not only does such exertion require an increase in blood flow to the muscles but the cold weather also increases the body's general requirements for heat and thus blood. Angina usually resolves with cessation of the strenuous activity and a moment by the hearth, but in those cases when the warning goes unheeded and the activity continues the prolonged deprivation of the overworked and undersupplied heart muscle can result in the myocardial death of a classic heart attack. Such a patient is managed in a slightly different manner than the acute coronary syndrome due to plaque rupture and blood clot (which often has its onset during sleep), for there is presumably no blood clot present to lyse with aspirin or tPA. Either type of patient can benefit from the effects of nitroglycerin, which both dilates the vessels supplying the heart and causes venous pooling which reduces the amount of fluid the heart must pump. Reduction of blood pressure and heart rate can also reduce the size of an infarct by decreasing the heart's demand for blood-borne sustenance. Nitroglycerin may have helped Mr. Griggs, but he had never had pain of this type before and so had proceeded to finish off both the driveway and a portion of his heart muscle.

Mr. Griggs had been admitted to the coronary care unit as an acute heart attack can result in death in a number of ways, the most common being a cardiac arrhythmia. This disruption of the heart's electrical impulses is analogous to a seizure. The flow of electricity over the surface of the heart begins with each beat in the sinoatrial node and passes smoothly throughout the remainder of the muscle, resulting in the ordered and concentric contraction of the heart's chambers. This electrical flow resembles a smooth glassy stream, and any focus of dead or dying tissue acts as a boulder thrusting up from the streambed with resultant eddies and ripples. The heart muscle can then begin to quiver rather than contract in concerted fashion, and there is a subsequent loss of forward blood flow. The condition can be immediately fatal and can occur with a heart attack of any size and so arrhythmia prevention is the main focus of management in acute heart attacks. It is these patients that are infrequently saved with CPR, but the definitive treatment of the condition is the delivery of an electric shock or "defibrillation." The delivery of such a shock can synchronize the flow of impulses and convert the stream from a raging rapid to its previous state of steady flow. Coronary care units are designed specifically with this complication in mind, and the EKG of every patient with an acute heart attack is monitored continuously in the days following the event. Although artificial EKG abnormalities can arise from activity of the chest wall muscles and many a patient has received a painful shock while brushing his teeth, the success of these units in general is inarguable and they are omnipresent in the country's hospitals. In fact, their success has led to the inappropriate use of acute coronary algorithms in patients dying of any cause with an unfortunate increase in work for the morticians who must disguise the resulting electrical burns. The difference between these situations lies in the fact that cardiac arrhythmias from acute heart attacks are short-lived, transient, and reversible while those occurring in dying cancer patients represent a final event from extensive systemic metabolic abnormalities and generally will not resolve with a single shock.

Mr. Griggs had suffered no problems during his stay in the CCU, although he did beat off one algorithm-induced nursing assault with his toothbrush. He was transferred to the wards just two days ago for a final tuning of his medications and was due for discharge after a treadmill test verified that he had no undersupplied heart muscle still poised on the brink of death. Heart muscle once dead cannot be recovered and will lie dormant, but heart muscle in the throes of strangulation can result in more arrhythmias and so must be sought out. Patients with evidence of persistent ischemia therefore undergo cardiac catheterization or even bypass surgery, but Mr. Griggs had needed no such extreme measures. In spite of his extensive testing and monitoring it is interesting that no one knew just how much of Mr. Griggs' heart had succumbed.

When Midlin saw Mr. Griggs' upright posture and low oximetry reading he began to suspect the source of the problem, and a quick listen with his stethoscope confirmed his suspicions. The crackling noises and wheezing in his lungs were the first manifestations of fluid backup and it was clear that Mr. Griggs was developing congestive heart failure. The fluid accumulating in the walls of his bronchial tubes was narrowing the air passages, and the resulting wheezing had been referred to in years past as "cardiac asthma." Enough of his heart muscle had died to affect the pumping of his heart and his current medications to lower blood pressure and reduce the circulating volume of fluid had been insufficient to ease the strain on the beleaguered left ventricle, and the fluid his heart was unable to pump was now filling his lungs. Midlin ordered a relatively expensive dose of Lasix without thinking and shortly after its injection Mr. Griggs' posture and oximetry readings improved.

Although the problem seemed to be straightforward and also to have resolved, Midlin was acutely aware that he was to meet the hypervigilant Sargent soon and so extended his list of orders to include a chest x-ray and an EKG for the sake of completeness. As he awaited the arrival of the various technicians with their wheeled machinery he dashed off a note in Mr. Griggs' chart intended at least in part as a reprimand for Aines. As he finished the technicians arrived, followed shortly by Sargent herself.

"I tucked that admission," she said, pulling up a chair and plopping into it. It was now almost 3 AM and she finally was beginning to look tired. "It was a babysitting job for an 18-year-old with strep throat. I did the admission note and orders for IV hydration and penicillin, but I decided not to do a testicular and rectal exam since his family was in the room. You can go past there when we're done and write your note and finish the exam."

Midlin was of sufficient experience to know not to express surprise at Sargent's thoroughness, but of course only she and Robbins performed such exams in patients admitted for unrelated issues. Midlin was of the opinion that these screening exams belonged in the clinics but as he felt indebted to Sargent already he agreed to her requests without comment. Attending physicians rarely contributed so much to late-night patient care and Midlin was grateful even though he knew Sargent had ulterior motives. Even at this late hour she was preparing her charts for Flynn's perusal in the morning.

While Midlin described Mr. Griggs' situation to Sargent the requested EKG strip and chest x-ray were brought to them at the nurses' station, both of which confirmed Midlin's initial assessment of the situation. The EKG showed no change from previous tracings, demonstrating only small 'Q' waves which were the result of a prior infarction and which would probably be present on Mr. Griggs' EKGs for the rest of his life. The chest x-ray also was consistent with early congestive heart failure as it demonstrated the spider web appearance of interstitial pulmonary edema. The fluid backing into the lungs was thickening the otherwise fine wisps of tissue throughout the lungs, but was not yet under such pressure as to fill the actual alveolar air sacs of the lungs (a phenomenon that would appear a dense white on x-ray and which would imply a much more serious degree of heart failure). Midlin was feeling quite proud of his accurate assessment and management when Sargent turned her attention to his abbreviated note in the chart. Although perfectly adequate in its description of the situation, Midlin could see by Sargent's expression that it would not suffice to impress Flynn on his arrival in the morning. She slid the chart across to him and with a nod indicated that he should once again take dictation from her.

There was little to add in the earlier sections of the note. Mr. Griggs' complaints, his exam findings, and his vital signs were not debatable and no corrections were required. Rather than list differential possibilities at the end of the note, however, Midlin had simply written "congestive heart failure" as no other such possibilities had seemed to exist. Sargent, however, wanted Flynn to see that she knew every possible cause of an "interstitial infiltrate" on chest x-ray and so recited a long list from memory. Incredibly and most likely due to the late hour, Sargent stumbled somewhere between hypersensitivity pneumonitis and chronic aspiration and was forced to consult one of her many pocket reference books.

"Of course!" she exclaimed after finding the appropriate page. "Lymphangioleiomyomatosis! How could I have forgotten?" With this she closed the book and stood, her night's work apparently at last at an end. But she had one last comment to indicate that sleep was only her secondary concern while

Flynn remained foremost in her mind.

"I will be around tomorrow morning to finish up some paperwork. Give me a call if you have any questions on rounds." And with this she at last departed for her uncomfortable call room, leaving Midlin to find his way upstairs to complete Sargent's supposedly incomplete admission.

Mr. Strickler was only eighteen years old, barely qualifying for the internal medicine service rather than the pediatric. This was just as well as he was spared sleeping in an undersized bed under balloons and murals of cartoon characters, and he further benefited from having doctors who eschewed the word "poo-poo" in their history-taking. Mr. Strickler would likely have survived in any case, however, as he had been admitted simply for hydration and antibiotics and would most likely be discharged in a matter of hours.

An exception to the usual rule of antibiotic overuse, streptococcal pharyngitis or "strep throat" remains exquisitely sensitive to penicillin despite its worldwide treatment with this drug for the last fifty years. Most bacteria exposed to the same antibiotic for extended periods will ultimately mutate and develop resistant strains, but like an old person refusing to learn personal computing the *Streptococcus pyogenes* bacterium has failed to alter its molecular overcoat in spite of the obvious survival advantages such a change would impart. The only potential for treatment failures thus lies in abscess formation or in development of such severe pharyngitis that pill swallowing is precluded, and this was the fate that had befallen Mr. Strickler. His painful inability to swallow had extended to liquids as well, and so he had presented to the ER with raging fevers, swollen nodes, and the dizziness that so often accompanies dehydration. Less than twenty-four hours of treatment would most likely see him well on the road to recovery, and Midlin approached the nurses' station expecting a minimal amount of documentation. At eighteen years old and with a straightforward illness, Midlin could not see how Mr. Strickler could provide the clinical fodder for more than a page-long admission note.

Upon opening the chart Midlin suffered what he would later remember as the emotional nadir of his internship, including even the ER debacle of his first day. He had grossly underestimated Sargent's enthusiasm in spite of his familiarity with her ways and found himself reading four pages of small script with no margins. She had listed Mr. Strickler's immunization history and all of the childhood illnesses he had suffered. His past medical history, free of hospitalizations and other significant events, was still a complete section listing such occurrences as ankle sprains and ingrown toenails. His family history included a description of the demise of every family member for the four preceding generations. His social history listed his habits (which were few) and his girlfriends (which were many) as well as his educational and employment history. The physical examination section went on for a complete page in spite of Sargent's omission of the testicular and rectal exams and included such descriptions as hair and nails, dentition and gums, and a survey of his freckles and other skin lesions. Lastly, Sargent had ordered so many laboratory tests that Midlin suspected Mr. Strickler would progress from dehydrated to thoroughly desiccated at the hands of the phlebotomists.

He couldn't do this, Midlin thought. If this were the standard to which doctors were held then he may as well give up right now. He could never perform on this level, not after years of training and with unlimited time to perform each patient evaluation. He couldn't see how Sargent had even had the time to physically write this admission note much less acquire all the information therein, and he certainly couldn't see himself ever accomplishing such a feat. His depression was such that he didn't even begin his own note, for he could see no potential benefit from a half-page intern's note added to the end of this medical *War and Peace*. With the clock reading 4 AM Midlin opted for two hours of sleep for both himself and Mr. Strickler, reasoning that every eventuality was accounted for and that Mr. Strickler's testicles would still be there in the morning. As Midlin climbed the stairs to bed, however, he felt as though Sargent had effectively removed his own.

CHAPTER 15

Midlin awakened from his short sleep with a start, not surprised to find himself both in the call room and completely unrefreshed. One glance at the clock on his pager told him he was only just in time for rounds and with this also came the realization that he had not had time to see his many patients prior to presenting them to Flynn. Dreading chastisement for his many omissions (particularly with regard to Mr. Strickler) he nevertheless flew down the stairs two at a time to join his fellow interns at the first floor nurses' station and so not compound his sins by being late. No such haste had been necessary as he found the others waiting idly and no evidence of Flynn's small but dominating presence.

The minutes dragged on with the typical agitation of the interns increasing as their time for note-writing was whittled away by Flynn's tardiness. Robbins had finally decided to take the aggressive step of paging the attending physician and had the phone in her hand when Flynn finally appeared, coming not down the hallway from the main entrance but rather emerging from Mr. Larkin's room behind them. Robbins hurriedly hung up the phone before her impatience had manifested itself on Flynn's pager.

Flynn nodded to the others and held out his hand to Midlin, the only intern whom he as yet had not formally met. With Sargent gone Robbins had clearly decided it was her job to supply an air of disapproval and so she remained somewhat aloof, but Aines and Oggler greeted Flynn with smiles and excitement and were obviously glad of the change in supervision. For once Oggler was not sweating visibly and Aines' head was not shaking.

The interns' agitation diminished further as rounds progressed, for none of them had ever seen the process conducted with such speed and efficiency. The discussion of each case was remarkably abbreviated, and there was no recitation of the various lists so dear to Sargent's heart. Midlin thought of how disappointed Sargent would be as Flynn never once asked to see the patients' charts or read the exhaustive differential possibilities Sargent had so carefully provided for him. He did nothing more than meet every patient and acquire a general sense of the mood in each room before moving on, and there was no time spent on physical examination whatsoever. Flynn never once produced a stethoscope and Midlin began to wonder if he even carried one (the medical equivalent of a priest without a cross). Flynn's interruptions were the exact opposite of Sargent's, intended to cut short the meandering of the relatively inexperienced interns rather than extending it. Midlin became quickly convinced that his brevity was an attempt to conceal his lack of solid medical knowledge and in spite of the levity Flynn brought to rounds Midlin began to miss Sargent dearly.

Robbins was resistant to this new approach and made no

attempt to modify her presentations. While Flynn clearly desired a one-sentence synopsis of each patient's course she was determined to provide a complete, formatted discussion of each case. Her first such presentation was sarcastically truncated by the time she began enumerating her first patients' many laboratory values, most of which were normal.

"Oh, Jesus, I'm sorry," said Flynn, interrupting her and feigning an awakening from sleep. "I've been thinking about sex for the last five minutes. Did I miss anything? Is anything actually wrong with this guy?"

Robbins began reading the list of problems she had compiled at the bottom of her progress note, and as she read the headings of constipation, insomnia, and back pain as well as every other incidental complaint her patient had expressed her voice and confidence began to dwindle. The patient's initial problem had resolved days ago and he was obviously ripe for discharge, and after a final sweeping glance at her list she sighed and concluded, "Well, no." Flynn entered the room, shook the patient's hand, and they were on the move again.

When they arrived at Mr. Griggs' room Midlin briefly took over Aines' presentation in order to recount the events of the night before. After about thirty seconds Flynn seemed to think the discussion was concluded and began to edge toward the room for a quick handshake, but Midlin like Robbins was not to be denied the opportunity to recite a list. While Flynn continued his subtle migration toward the door Midlin extolled the exhaustive list Sargent had dictated the night before. At first Flynn's face showed only boredom, but when Midlin reached the bottom of the list Flynn finally was interested, and he took two fast steps forward to rejoin the group.

"...and lymphangioleiomyomatosis," concluded Midlin, raising his gaze with a satisfied look that froze on his face as he saw Flynn's expression. The leprechaun-like face still was overtly sarcastic but also showed a hint of seriousness that

Midlin had never suspected existed in him.

"You really think this post-infarction patient with interstitial edema responsive to furosemide has lymphangioleiomyomatosis?" he asked, obviously sure of the answer.

Midlin fully realized what he had been vaguely aware of the night before when Sargent had picked this entity off the bottom of a printed differential list: he had never heard of lymphangioleiomyomatosis before and couldn't even spell it correctly, much less provide any information about it. "Well…no," he answered.

"Riiight," said Flynn. "Do you even know what it is?"

Midlin realized he was caught and saw no need to prolong their collective agony. "No," he said, hoping that Flynn would at least appreciate his brevity.

"It is a disease characterized by proliferation of smooth muscle cells in the lungs which results in cyst formation and interstitial prominence on chest x-ray. It can be associated with spontaneous pneumothorax and chylous effusions and is almost always seen in the setting of the phakomatosis syndrome tuberous sclerosis. It most likely is due to the tropic effects of estrogen on these cells, and so your patient would be the first male afflicted in several hundred years of recorded medical history. I think we'll stick with the CHF as the most likely problem."

Flynn did not pause to see the effects of his speech and had returned from meeting Mr. Griggs before Midlin had fully recovered. Midlin was forced to face the fact that Flynn knew infinitely more about lymphangioleiomyomatosis than where to find it on a differential diagnosis list, and rather than concealing his lack of knowledge he was simply too smart to waste time considering it as a possibility.

The team arrived at Mr. Jackson's room and in response to the many posted warning signs all began to don their personalized pig masks in preparation for entry. Flynn had no mask and made no move to acquire one.

"What's the deal here?" he asked, and Midlin nervously began recounting Mr. Jackson's story, getting only so far as cough, lymphadenopathy and chronic shortness of breath before he was interrupted.

"Is he black?" asked Flynn abruptly.

"Well, African-American, yes," said Midlin, knowing Robbins' love of politically correct phrasing and not wanting to offend. She had been known to omit race altogether in her patient presentations.

"His race is a little more relevant than his citizenship here," retorted Flynn. "I take it that he is both. Is there any reason to suspect tuberculosis here? Is he an immigrant? Is he a nursing home patient? HIV positive? Otherwise institutionalized? Retarded? Oh, sorry, mentally challenged?"

Midlin for once began to question the need for the extensive testing ordered the night before, but he was unwilling to relinquish his position out of deference to Sargent's tutelage.

"Well, no, but he *could* have it all the same," he answered somewhat lamely, and then tried to rally even more lamely with, "or he could have tuberculosis *and* cancer."

"Yes, and he *could* also be the second male in history with lymphangioleiomyomatosis. Come on, a black guy with chronic shortness of breath, cough, and mediastinal lymphadenopathy? What's he really got?"

Flynn's phrasing made the answer as obvious to Midlin as it was to Flynn himself, and the answer sprang from Midlin's lips almost without thought. "He has sarcoidosis," he said, finally recovering a little confidence.

"Riiight. Cancel all that stuff you ordered so Mr. Jackson can pay his mortgage, send him home on a steroid taper and set him up in my clinic for a month from now."

Flynn entered the room and shook Mr. Jackson's hand without a mask, and in so doing became the first human visage the man had seen for sixteen hours.

Midlin began his apologies with regard to Mr. Strickler before they had even arrived at the nursing station outside his room. He offered stammering, lame excuses for the absence of his own admission note as well as the absence of testicular and rectal exams by citing workload and a need for sleep, but Flynn seemed completely unconcerned. Flynn's interest was piqued, however, when he opened the chart and saw Sargent's four-page note and he emitted a soft whistle that Midlin completely misinterpreted.

"I know," Midlin said, experiencing awe and chagrin all over again at the sight of the document. "Impressive, isn't it? I don't know how she does it."

"Are you kidding? Don't you see what this is? Whoever wrote this note is completely unable to make a decision, completely unable to separate relevant facts from irrelevant details. It's the work of an idiot."

Midlin was shocked to hear his esteemed mentor referred to in this manner and could only mumble, unwilling to express agreement.

"Come on," said Flynn, pressing his point in spite of Midlin's reluctance. "When you first heard of this admission how much did you expect to write?"

Midlin was forced to provide the honest answer in spite of the fact that he knew it would prove Flynn's point. "Well, one page, I guess."

"Riiight," said Flynn again. "I want you to write half that much today and get this guy out of here when he can swallow and before someone does something awful to him." Flynn was preparing to close the chart when his gaze fell on the document's date and time in the upper left corner. He paused.

"Didn't you say Sargent told you to do a testicular and rectal exam on this guy last night?" he asked, and Midlin was once again overwhelmed with shame at this obvious omission.

"Yes, but like I said I was…"

Flynn mercifully cut him off. "So you were supposed to go in there at four in the morning and feel this eighteen-year-old's nuts and stick a finger up his ass for no good reason?"

In spite of its crudity Flynn's statement was obviously accurate. "Well, yes…" answered Midlin, unsure if he was in trouble or not.

"Good thing you didn't," said Flynn, briefly allaying Midlin's fears. But then Flynn continued and gave birth to a whole new set of worries. "I'd say if you'd taken your lawyer and six witnesses you would still probably be in jail this morning." Flynn closed the chart and moved on without even a handshake for Mr. Strickler. They all followed along with Midlin bringing up the rear, thankful both for his freedom and for the extra sleep he had gotten the night before.

At the incredible hour of 10 AM they arrived back at Mr. Larkin's room. Midlin had begun organizing his presentation on Mr. Larkin several patients back and then had attempted to mentally edit it to under an hour. He knew Flynn would have no patience for an enumeration of Mr. Larkin's many complications when there was no unifying diagnosis to present. He began noncommittally and tried to gloss over this obvious deficiency.

"Well, we're not really sure what brought Mr. Larkin in, but since he's been here…"

As usual, Midlin was cut off in mid-sentence. "You're kidding? Was his HIV test negative?" Flynn asked, his eyebrows raised in surprise.

There was shocked silence. No HIV test had ever been ordered on Mr. Larkin and the very suggestion seemed ridiculous. It had never occurred to a single house officer caring for the man in the last five months. In spite of the fact that he was only one of fifteen people to whom the idea of AIDS had never occurred Midlin was currently the responsible intern and so was expected to speak on the issue.

"We've never gotten an HIV test on him. He's a seventy-two year old man who..."

Flynn was by now used to finishing Midlin's sentences for him. "...Who goes to Thailand for six months a year with his army buddies to screw as many hookers as his limited budget allows. Or haven't you listened to those stories? I admit this will break my personal rule, since Mr. Larkin will be the first case of heterosexual, non-IV-drug abuser, non-transfusion AIDS I have ever seen in spite of what the media wants you to believe. There are supposedly some new strains in the Far East that can be transmitted that way, though, and I think if anybody would get one it would be your buddy there." Flynn looked around the group and saw only mute, embarrassed looks not entirely due to his choice of language. He realized his point was made. "Just order it," he said, and promptly left the ward without basking in his success. He had diagnosed Mr. Larkin in less than an hour of casual chat with no examination and no testing and events would of course prove him completely correct. When presented with the positive result the next day Flynn would only give a disinterested shrug, for he would have been as surprised to be told the sky was blue.

Midlin was preparing to leave for the day, having finished the discharge paperwork for both Mr. Strickler and Mr. Jackson. After all the precautions that had been taken the night before Mr. Jackson was pleasantly surprised to discover he wasn't really very sick. The presence of masked and gowned nurses tends to convince a patient that his symptoms are the first yet described in what will become a worldwide epidemic and that he will die before the illness is even given a name. The news of his upcoming discharge was thus welcome, and Mr. Jackson's mood would further improve when he began his course of steroids. The cessation of his medication would coincide with the arrival of his massive hospital bill, however, and so his elation would (as with most happiness) prove transitory. Midlin put the finishing touches on the five-dollar prescription which was all that had ever been required in Mr. Jackson's case, and just as he did so the overhead paging system bellowed the news of the hospital's latest emergency.

Such announcements were made both over the loudspeakers and on the "code" pagers distributed to the house officers on call. The code pagers guaranteed the presence of at least three interns at such events no matter what the hour, but during the day the excitement could bring any number of curious onlookers drawn by the loudspeaker. Doctors at all levels of training would come running in the hope of demonstrating their superior knowledge or the inadequacies of others, a fact that explained Sargent's presence at most of these often-tragic gatherings.

Midlin was balancing his desire to sleep with his desire to witness the resuscitation, an event considered by most interns to be the Grand Prix of medical experiences in spite of the fact that almost all "codes" amounted only to the intubation, catheterization, and electrocution of an already-dead patient. It was the fact that the ER was on the way to the parking lot that had mostly convinced him to attend, but then the sight of Oggler trundling slowly by with a code pager on his belt was the clinching factor in his decision. Even with a late start he would beat Oggler the tortoise to the scene by a good five minutes, possibly even in time to make a contribution.

Mr. and Mrs. Luckner had been dining at a nearby restaurant in celebration of their fiftieth anniversary. They had enjoyed dessert and coffee, paid their hefty bill, and then had begun the trip home on a road that ran right past the hospital. As they approached the turnoff to the hospital's ER they were talking animatedly in spite of their many years together and then suddenly Mrs. Luckner had slumped silently against her husband's shoulder. Mr. Luckner, showing a rare presence of mind, had run the light at the intersection and raced to the front doors of the ER, followed closely by a black-and-white intent on meeting all its monthly ticket quotas in one fell swoop. The police arrived to find Mr. Luckner struggling with his wife's limp body and incredibly assisted rather than cited him. Further adding to their good fortune the uniquely intelligent triage nurse had hit the emergency "code" alarm without requesting so much as a single signature and within two minutes of her collapse Mrs. Luckner was on a gurney and doctors from all corners of the hospital were rushing to her aid.

Midlin, Sargent, and Flynn all arrived breathlessly and simultaneously. While obviously profoundly aware of one another's presence Flynn and Sargent exchanged barely a nod at the door to the room, and Midlin saw Sargent barge over the threshold while Flynn drew up and paused before Mr. Luckner. Mr. Luckner saw the questioning look on Flynn's face and began his story.

"We were driving by when she just collapsed…" he began, and Flynn had already heard enough. He entered the room just seconds behind Sargent.

The simple mnemonic "ABC" applies not only to CPR performed by lay persons in health clubs and restaurants but also to resuscitations performed in hospitals. The difference lies mainly in the available equipment; the "A" for "airway" amounts to only a jaw thrust to move the tongue for a lay person but in the hospital it implies endotracheal intubation. Similar differences exist in the subsequent steps of "breathing" and "circulation" but their order remains effectively unchanged, and in spite of the sophistication of hospital surroundings most doctors rely on that unforgettable mnemonic to guide their actions in critical situations.

As dictated by the traditional algorithm Sargent was at the head of the bed, fumbling to secure Mrs. Luckner's airway with a curved plastic oral insert prior to intubating her. Midlin watched as Flynn walked instead to the far side of the room and in one smooth motion turned on the portable defibrillator, kicked the cart across the room and snatched up the metal-surfaced paddles. He paused only long enough to catch Sargent's eye and menacingly raised the paddles over Mrs. Luckner's chest. This second seemed to last a minute as Flynn and Sargent confronted one another, Sargent supported in her attention to the airway by the age-old mnemonic but Flynn backed by several hundred joules aimed at Mrs. Luckner and anyone else in physical contact with her. Sargent realized that Flynn would welcome the opportunity to include her in his therapeutic endeavors and so ultimately pushed her wheeled chair back a foot, glaring at her unorthodox nemesis as she did so. She was already mentally composing her official letter of complaint as Flynn placed the paddles on Mrs. Luckner's chest without pausing to lubricate them or to open her shirt.

Defibrillation paddles and the portable electrical source to which they are attached can display a crude EKG tracing for emergency diagnosis, but Flynn did not hesitate even the necessary second for this objective confirmation. He simply depressed the red buttons on the paddles and watched with satisfaction as widespread muscle contraction caused Mrs. Luckner's body to arch briefly off the bed. Only then did Flynn rest the paddles quietly on her chest to view her EKG tracing, and when he saw the normal QRS complexes marching regularly across the screen he simply dropped the paddles to the floor and turned away. He left the room almost immediately, pausing only to give Mr. Luckner's arm an encouraging but silent squeeze. He never did see Mrs. Luckner's eyelids flutter as she regained consciousness, and Mrs. Luckner saw only Sargent's face as the latter returned to her position to pursue a now-unnecessary intubation. In another thirty seconds Mrs. Luckner would have begun to suffer irreversible brain damage, and Sargent had been prepared to spend that time fumbling in her mouth with a sterilized shoehorn. Mrs. Luckner's appropriate and barely audible words of thanks were thus delivered to an entirely inappropriate recipient.

CHAPTER 16

Midlin lay in bed lazily, having awakened before his alarm as he had gone to bed in the late afternoon the day before. He only now had time to consider and assimilate the lessons he had learned, and he was somewhat overwhelmed by the intensity of his single day with Flynn and all that it implied.

There was no question that list memorization was an important part of medical education, but Midlin realized now that it was only the beginning. Appropriate decision-making had to be based on a total familiarity with the human body and the processes that affect it, with differential lists and algorithms playing a supplementary and not primary role. A view of the situation as a whole was first required with the smaller details identified and acknowledged but only specifically addressed as they related to the larger picture. Midlin's head swam as he pondered this new way of thinking, and as he considered what he hoped would be a change in his approach to medicine he was grateful to realize that at least his efforts at list memorization were not wasted. He was glad to have that solid basis for decisions but at the same time was distressed to realize he had so much more to learn. He still, for example, could not spell lymphangioleiomyomatosis.

Midlin's reverie was abruptly interrupted as the silence of the morning was shattered by the sound of Tees' TV. A common enough occurrence, today the noise would have far-reaching implications. Because Midlin's current consideration of Flynn and his ability to view the forest rather than the trees coincided with the blaring of Tees' TV, Midlin suddenly had a flash of insight that proved to him he would be a worthy disciple of Flynn's.

Tees was independently wealthy. Tees had unlimited energy and seemed to require little sleep. Tees frequently absented himself from work, even without the insistence of the administration. Tees was frequently agitated and inappropriate. Tees had suffered a subarachnoid hemorrhage with no evidence of an underlying aneurysm. Taken as individual events and attributes these facts were not particularly suggestive, but when viewed as a whole in a dispassionate and distanced fashion they added up to one inevitable conclusion. Tees was on drugs, probably cocaine.

Midlin was convinced immediately when the thought entered his head, as convinced as Flynn had been that Mr. Larkin had AIDS or that Mrs. Luckner had been suffering from a cardiac arrhythmia. He lay for several minutes listening to Tees' TV trumpet the opening themes of *Good Morning America* as he debated the appropriate course of action.

Foremost of Midlin's emotions was anger. He had covered for Tees when he was absent, backed him when vilified and worried about him when hospitalized. Now he realized that all these efforts amounted to was the enabling of a drug habit. He tried to look past this anger to decide on an objective response but it was difficult, and he further realized the importance of objectivity since the decision as to how to handle things would be his and his alone. He was the only one who knew the truth and he had been the one most directly affected. In addition, as convinced as he was of the truth it would be impossible to prove, for cocaine is rapidly eliminated and therefore difficult to identify with drug testing. He hoped he could appeal to Tees' friendship when the upcoming confrontation took place. With a final surge of rage at being placed in this awkward position Midlin rose from bed, dressed, and crossed the hallway between their apartments.

Midlin drove to work that morning mulling over his conversation with Tees. Tees had neither denied nor verified Midlin's accusations initially but he did listen silently as Midlin outlined his ideas for managing the problem. Midlin had suggested that Tees excuse himself from the rest of the internship year, pointing out that with Tees' recent hospitalizations a declaration of "medical reasons" would most likely suffice as justification. Tees could use that time to enter into a private and secret treatment program and most likely would be ready to return to medical training the coming year. Midlin had made only veiled reference to what he would do if Tees refused, but fortunately Tees was grateful for Midlin's friendship and discretion and so the aggressive confrontation Midlin had dreaded had not occurred. As Midlin left Tees had simply said, "I'll think about it," which was all the admission Midlin needed to hear to verify his conclusions. As Midlin took the hospital exit he noted his speed was increasing steadily in spite of successive reductions in the speed limit, and at first he blamed this on his irritation with Tees. As he hustled into the hospital from the parking lot, however, he recognized the real reason for his haste. He was anxious to work with Flynn.

THE END

Printed in the United States
19756LVS00001B/430

9 781413 709797